OUR
FRAIL
DISORDERED
LIVES

MARY M. SCHMIDT

ISBN: 978-1-4834-8510-2 (sc)
ISBN: 978-1-4834-8509-6 (e)

Library of Congress Control Number: 2018905180

Lulu Publishing Services rev. date: 5/10/2018

In memory of Ann C. Crispin

1950–2013

1

It's never easy hearing that the boss wants to see you. Right away. "Drop what you're doing; bring me that contract. Now!" Even if you think you have done your work well, you know in advance that he's never satisfied.

Especially if your boss is the devil himself.

In the beginning, he had been Lucifer, the most radiant of all created beings. Now he was known as Satan, Lord of the Flies, Father of Lies. Old Scratch—only to his fellow demons. He was no more the beautiful Lucifer but a fat, bald, ugly little man with a potbelly and way too many warts.

What a temper he had.

Satan's receptionist asked the demon Roach to have a seat in the waiting room. This was always the way it was done. You had to be on time—but Satan, not so much. His time was valuable. Yours not nearly as much as his. Don't forget that.

Plus the waiting area was dirty and depressing. There were two vending machines, one selling lukewarm soda pop, the other stale candy, and neither had worked for eons. Stains covered the floor and walls. You had to take care how you sat on the couch since the upholstery was torn with springs sticking out of it. It was always too hot or cold in here.

The receptionist was an eyesore. She was not even a demon but a damned soul. Roach wondered what she did in her life to end up in a place like this. It was said that she gave birth in a fleabag motel and left the baby to freeze in the dumpster. Roach could believe it. And then there was the noise, the constant whining of the damned souls, the mocking laughter of demons like himself.

Also it smelled bad. Someone in the Upper World once spoke of "the smoke of Satan." He certainly was right. This whole area reeked of Satan's eternal cigars.

Now, you might think, this being the executive suite of Hell, it would at least be clean and freshly painted. But oh, no! Satan was a cheapskate. A lowly demon like Roach was hardly in a position to offer suggestions. When Asmodeus hinted that having an exterminator or cleaning crew might help, Satan reminded him of the class of people with whom he was obligated to deal.

"I'm not rolling out a red carpet for that trash," he snarled.

Roach looked over the contract he had with him. All was in order, signed, and initialed in every place by himself and the potential damned soul, witnessed and notarized as needed. So Satan ought to be pleased.

There was a buzz, and the receptionist told Roach he could go on in now. This hardly meant Satan was ready. He was on the phone, as usual, chewing another demon out. "Oh, really?" he asked. "My heart just bleeds! Look—you tell him to get it done by noon tomorrow or else! And he knows what *or else* is. And I don't want to hear one more of his lame excuses! I want results!"

He cut off the call. "Do you have it with you?" he asked Roach.

"Yes, Great One."

"Let's see it."

Satan thumbed through the pages of fine-print legalese. "Who did you say this fool was?" he asked.

"Lawrence Paul Kavanaugh Junior."

"And what does Lawrence Paul Kavanaugh Junior do for a living?"

"He's an attorney."

"Is he now?" Satan murmured. "How impressive. And how do you know that, Roach?"

"Well, he said so."

"He … said so," Satan muttered, studying the signature page. "I see. Isn't that profound."

Suddenly, Satan jumped up and heaved the contract at Roach.

"What a piece of junk this is! And you, Roach! You ought to be ashamed of yourself!"

"What did I do wrong?"

"You call this a contract for the sale of an immortal soul?"

"Kavanaugh says he doesn't think he's got one."

"Boloney! That's what they all say. Pick up those papers. Put them back in order!"

"But …"

"But nothing. He said he was an attorney, and you took his word for it? You did nothing to verify it? You never thought to consult the state bar association?"

Roach was at a loss for words.

"Even if I did not know for a fact that Kavanaugh was never admitted to any bar association, that Kavanaugh is too stupid to pass the exam, I could have told you as much just by looking at this mess you made."

Satan slammed the pages down beside a much larger contract. "Now this," he said as he pounded his fist on a larger document, "represents the sale of the soul of a real attorney. Notice the difference?"

Roach began to sweat.

"Kavanaugh is a fraud. A con man. Unable to become what he wants to be, he fakes it. So all he did was sign pretty much the basic boilerplate contract. He wants a long and prosperous career pulling the wool over other people's eyes. Including yours, I might add. He just does not want to get caught by any fact-checker. He doesn't want to go to prison. So he goes to Hell. What a pathetic, putrid little soul. Whereas, look here."

Satan tossed over the other contract. It was huge and covered with cross-outs, corrections, and the required number of initials and seals. Roach gasped when he saw the signature.

"That's right—the most brilliant and ruthless legal mind in Manhattan. Is he accepting the boilerplate? Certainly not. He specifies everything. Everything! The firm of his choice. His salary and bonuses. His penthouse, his summerhouse, ski condo, his cars, boats, and jets. His wife—she must be submissive, faithful, and has to look the other way when he is not so to her. He must not catch any nasty diseases from his outside activities. His children: a minimum of seven, five of whom must be boys. The boys have to look like him. On the other hand, the girls have to be beautiful. None of his children may have any sort of mental or physical defect. Sexually, all his children have to be heteronormative and at the proper time will marry spouses of whom he approves. He even has his life span in here: minimum one hundred years. Oh, and he has to die quickly and painlessly, no long illness or dementia. He must live to see twelve grandchildren and four great-grands. All restrictions on his children apply to subsequent generations. Roach, do you see the difference here? Can you imagine the fight I had to put up to get his soul in here? He acted like he thought I was Santa Claus. There are no loopholes here, nothing I can exploit! Whereas souls like Kavanaugh's? A dime a dozen!"

Satan sighed and picked up the Kavanaugh contract. "Next time … if there is a next time … would you please verify everything they tell you? They lie, Roach. Just like us. This one lied, and you fell for it. That's what he does. So where does that leave me? With a binding contract, sad to say, meaning I'm stuck for all eternity with this nobody. Another nobody who thinks I'm running some sort of Club Med down here."

"I'm … sorry, O Great One," Roach said.

"You ought to be," Satan said. "Go. Think of a few ways you can redeem yourself. Though I doubt you are able to do so."

Roach was quick to leave.

Satan leaned back and sighed. On his computer screen, he opened up the file of the real attorney whose soul he had won.

Now this was interesting. Unlike Kavanaugh, he neglected to specify that he'd never get caught in any wrongdoing. He had taken that for granted. There was that human weakness again. Pride. *It can't happen to me; I'm too important.* The worst of the deadly sins, the taproot of the Tree of the Knowledge of Good and Evil.

So he tempted fate and had just gotten away with a massive tax fraud. Or had he?

Satan imagined his star client doing a perp walk in front of all the world's media. He'd be forced to trade his pinstripes for an orange jumpsuit, all by his own doing. Yes, indeed, by his own free will.

"Why not?" Satan asked himself. After all, since "I won't get caught no matter what I do" was not specified as part of his contract, it was not binding, was it?

Here was a loophole ready to exploit. Of course, the idea came thanks to Roach, but damned if Roach would get any credit for it. Satan got back on his phone and explained that he was a concerned citizen with an anonymous tip. The wheels were set in motion, and for the first time in ages, Satan tossed back his horned head and laughed.

2

There were times, like right now, one had to get the hell out of Hell. Roach still had his duties, his list of damned souls to torture. They could wait. Roach retreated to the Upper World.

It was not unusual for demons to venture into the Upper World. However, as cheap as Satan was with his decor, he wanted his technical department to be on par with whatever was in the Upper World. He had a big advantage in the demon called Scorch, who ran the IT department. Some called Scorch the Patron Demon of the Internet.

Demons in their natural form are invisible. In their invisible form, each has a wart on the end of his nose, which is actually a GPS and communications device for Satan to get hold of him and call him back to Hell if he's needed. (That was how Satan summoned Roach back with the Kavanaugh contract.) Often, though, demons will take on visible form to communicate with, or hoodwink, those who have no idea about who or what they are.

Roach took on the visible form of a loser, an older white male down on his luck. This was a shabby part of town where he had landed, and he did not want to be conspicuous. That was part of the approach. You did not want to be too ugly, or people would stare at you. Not too attractive, or people would remember you.

However, Roach did not want to look so ruined that people would think he was homeless. He had tried that before. Some misguided souls tried to offer him money, food, or a place to sleep. Roach found that infuriating.

Roach was satisfied at his appearance in the mirror behind the bar.

No one would look at him twice. He sipped his whiskey. Many times, he'd swallowed better.

The bartender was conversing with another loser. Roach, still having his powers, not only heard what they said but did a deep scan of that only other patron of the bar. What a sad sack. Ulcers. Bad arteries too. He was telling the bartender his unemployment had run out. He was forced to live in his wife's mother's basement. He could not get along with the old bat, but where could he go? Even a rented room in a stranger's house was more than he could afford.

The bartender asked, "Did you try for Social Security disability?"

"Yeah. They turned me down, said I could still work."

"Why not appeal it?"

Sad Sack shook his head. "Whole thing's crazy."

Roach sent him a thought: *The river is just a block away. Why not jump off the bridge? Just think: the biggest splash you will ever make. And no more mother-in-law.*

After a while, the other man paid for his drink and wandered out. Roach gazed into his own drink and muttered, "I hate him."

"Excuse me?" the bartender asked as he wiped the man's place clean.

"Oh, nothing, nothing," Roach said. He offered up his glass and said, "Hit me again."

"You got it."

Again, Roach gazed into his drink and thought of how much he hated Satan. Really hated him, with a white-hot undying hatred. It had been so for ages, but what really sealed it was *that incident.*

Now, those in the Upper World could not simply stroll into Hell. The barriers that demons could cross were impossible for those known as the still-living. But there was that one time …

Two persons, one still-living, one a spirit, were permitted to cross the barrier and go all the way through the depths of Hell. Why? Both were poets. Such a special breed. One was writing an account of all he saw. That was Dante, the Florentine. The other was his guide. That was Virgil, the Roman.

Now, Satan had his own ideas, and he had their tour planned out in advance. What they could and could not see. To whom they could and could not speak. Which damned souls and demons they could interview.

And Roach? He was not on the approved list. He was nowhere near it. Not good enough, not scary enough, whatever!

Roach had laid a curse on that so-called *Divine Comedy*. He wanted it never to be published—or, if it was, to sell so poorly it was immediately forgotten. No such luck. It was still around to this day, in fancy illustrated editions, translated into every language there could possibly be. And none of these editions featured any mention of Roach.

Oh, how he hated Satan over that. And he knew Satan hated him too. That's why he kept getting set up for failure with all these lame assignments. Satan was never pleased with his work. But where else could he go? How could he get himself thrown out of Hell? There was no place worse for him. Or how could he die? He was stuck with immortality.

In the Great Hall of Pandemonium, there were several *aulae* (lecture halls) named after the most prominent damned souls. Judas Iscariot was the big one into which all citizens of Hell could fit. It was only for the most urgent occasions.

Roach sighed, remembering all the lectures in the Adolph Hitler aula he'd been forced to endure. Sometimes there would be a screening of *The Exorcist*, followed by a group discussion.

Pazuzu got all the praise. Roach got ignored. "Roach?" Satan once called on him. "Do you have anything to add?"

When Roach could not think of anything, Satan mocked him before the assembly. "That's because a real, live exorcist would have Roach jumping out of his scaly skin. Whereas our friend Pazuzu can fight tooth and nail." Laugher followed. What was never said was that Pazuzu lost the fight and was left with a case of PTSD and a phobia of stairs.

Whatever. Roach was certain he'd never be able to pull off an actual possession, so he did not pay attention during these boring mandatory lectures.

"Now," said Satan. "Since we are on the topic of possession of humans, why is it not done more frequently? Any thoughts? I see a hand up in back. Lamia?"

"Because it's difficult."

"Ah. And why is that so?"

"Because humans have free will."

"Very good. I see some of you are actually thinking. Roach ought to try that." Satan wrote *free will* on the board. "That means they can tell us no. They can refuse us. They can even resist us. To put a human's free will on override is always a challenge." Satan thought for a minute. "But worth it!"

Then Satan continued his usual lecture.

"What is rule one? I believe Beelzebub knows."

"Never tell your victim your real name."

Satan wrote that on the board. "Excellent!" he said. "And why not?"

"Because if they can name you, they have power over you."

Lamia giggled. "Or your real credit card number either!" Satan reminded her this was a serious matter.

"Find their weakness, and work with it. Sink your talons into the soft dry rot inside them. Why destroy one when you can destroy thousands! Millions!" Roach never joined in the applause.

While the bartender was in the washroom, Roach snuck out without paying and vanished into a crowd outside. There were many police present, so Roach felt he should leave quickly. Cops spooked him. Still, he found a pretty woman and asked her what was going on.

"Oh, it's terrible!" she said. "A man committed suicide, jumped off the bridge. The EMT fished him out, but he was already dead."

"Too bad," Roach muttered and crept away. What was worse, he knew it was his own doing and he'd never get any thanks. He hated Satan so much he'd like to ram that cigar down his throat. Or kick his sore spot under his tail, where the archangel Michael had delivered the final blow. It never really healed.

No one noticed that suddenly there was nothing where an ordinary down-on-his-luck man used to be. Roach felt an alarm in his wart. "Roach?" It was his supervisor. "I've got at least fifty pedophiles here, and they all have to be impaled. Where are you?"

"Tell them to go screw themselves," Roach muttered.

"What? Roach, you're breaking up. What did you say?"

"And tell the asshole you work for to go thou and do likewise. Roach over and out."

It hurt, but Roach tore his wart off, threw it to the ground, and crushed it with his hoof. He was free now. Here he was, in the Upper World, with all his demonic powers intact and no one to tell him what to do. He spread his wings and let an air current bear him gently above the scene of chaos. As he drifted, he let a Sinatra song go through his mind. "I Did It My Way." From now on, it would be Roach's anthem.

3

ScorchIT@inferno.org: Wazzup, bro?

Roach@hellraiser.com: I went rogue. You got a problem with that?

ScorchIT@inferno.org: No, but Old Scratch sure as hell does. He sent all his bounty hunters to the Upper World after you. You know that?

Roach@hellraiser.com: That's why I'm laying low.

ScorchIT@inferno.org: He's beyond mad. Saying what you did is unprecedented in the annals of Hell.

Roach@hellraiser.com: That's just tough.

ScorchIT@inferno.org: He's a lot madder that you called him an asshole.

Roach@hellraiser.com: ROTFL

ScorchIT@inferno.org: Seriously, bro. Watch your back.

Roach@hellraiser.com: Appreciate it, battle buddy.

Roach, in the human form of a haggard old woman, logged off the computer in the public library. Indeed, the past few weeks in the Upper World had been hard. He knew about the bounty hunters. On more than one occasion, they almost had him. He had been in his natural invisible form. In a human form, he was virtually impossible for them to track down.

And there was the problem. He'd hurt himself so badly in ripping off his tracking device, there was a big red hole on his nose. That made him ugly enough to be memorable. Not good.

Roach cursed when he saw his many images in the mirror. Even his good-looking avatars showed the ugly defect.

"If they think Satan is Santa Claus, they'll think I'm Rudolph," he muttered and confined himself to looking like unloved, lost, ugly people. He hoped it was temporary. The spot seemed to be healing, but it was taking forever.

At least his fellow demon Scorch had his back. Scorch was a genius with computers, not just in Hell, but he could hack into anything in the Upper World and leave no trace. Thus, they could stay in touch. He and Scorch went way back.

The homely old woman picked up her many shopping bags, left the library, and went to wait for the bus. He and Scorch went so far back they'd been friends since before time began.

Then Satan split with the Creator, and they cast their lot with Satan. Immediately, things went downhill. Both were drafted into Satan's army as buck privates.

They did nothing but complain. The food, the accommodations were terrible. Everything was hurry up and wait. But Satan promised them things would change once the battle was won. After that, they'd live like princes.

Roach and Scorch believed him.

Word came down that the general commanding the opposing army was the archangel Michael. That caused hilarity in the barracks. If the Creator seriously expected to win, why didn't he pick his general from a more powerful choir of angels? After all, their leader was Lucifer, the superior of all created beings. The victory was so close they could taste it.

Again, Roach and Scorch believed Satan.

Then the battle came. Roach and Scorch were way in the rear. There was little they could see through the fog of war. Then Beelzebub came at them. "Move it, you bastards! To the front! Go! Go! Go!"

Roach and Scorch, their weapons ready, ran into a blinding haze. Everywhere, there were screaming, wounded demons and flaming vehicles. It occurred to them they were expendable. And that this battle was not going as planned.

Only then did they have their first and only look at Michael. They were inches away from him. What little hair they had stood on end. They screamed, turned, and ran, but the ground opened up beneath them.

"Oh shit!" they cried out as they both started their long fall.

They lost track of how long the fall took, but at one point, Satan was falling a lot faster past them, gripping his rear and shrieking.

"You had that coming. You lied to us," Roach called after him.

"Fat lot of good that will do us," Scorch advised him.

Anyhow, that was how far back Roach and Scorch went. They were pals, and they'd had a few good times in the Upper World, with Scorch creating and spreading computer viruses. But the fun was over now. This was serious.

Roach had to get back to the crappy boarding house where he was staying. The bus was late. It was getting cold and dark.

Traffic stopped for a red light. Roach was aware of one of the drivers, a woman, staring at him. There were two children in the back seat.

"What are you looking at, toots?" he snarled. The light changed, and she was quick to leave.

4

Kathleen Kavanaugh was one of those women who are easily rattled.

She was always worried about so many things. Larry and the children, of course, but also the house, the car, just about anything. Especially, she worried about people who just weren't right.

Kathleen had no empathy for the mentally ill, because she believed that there was no such thing as mental illness. There was, instead, a certain moral weakness. So-called insane people needed to snap out of it. Kathleen was known to make fun of them, when in fact she was afraid of them.

Larry had done so much to provide her with everything she wanted. They had a good-enough house on Split Tree Circle. Yet it was said there was one oddity on every block. Floyd Ferguson, whom she called Flakey, lived across the street and a few doors down. Apparently, he had no family. He used to live with his mother, but she was long gone. He had a facial tic and a speech defect. His house, unlike the others here, was not especially well tended.

He did not cut his grass unless someone (usually Kathleen) called the county and complained. He was strange, and Kathleen was more than a bit afraid of him. Flakey Ferguson had never done anything illegal or threatening, to Kathleen's knowledge, but he unnerved her anyway. There was no telling what a person like that might do.

"Why is he even allowed to live here?" she once asked Larry.

"Who knows?" Larry shrugged. Kathleen avoided Flakey and kept the kids inside when he was in his yard.

"Kathleen, you worry too much," Larry told her. "Ferguson's

harmless. Why don't you take one of those yellow pills everybody's taking?"

But Kathleen refused to use tranquillizers and looked down on those who did. Kathleen was a strong person.

Which did not mean that she didn't get rattled. Especially today, with that apparition at the bus stop. She had never seen anyone so creepy as the old woman waiting there. Jeanine had spotted the creature first and said, "Mommy, what happened to that lady?"

Kathleen could not help but stare and jumped when the old woman shouted at her. She was so rattled she would have rear-ended the car in front of her had the light not turned green.

"What happened to her nose?" Jeanine asked. "Why is there a patch on it?"

"I really don't know, dear."

"Maybe she has leeprosy," Bobby said. "Her nose fell off, and she doesn't want anybody to know."

"Bobby, please. That's not nice," his mother urged him.

"Maybe her eyeballs are going to fall out next. Right at the bus stop. Plop, plop."

"Bobby!"

"What's leeprosy?" Jeanine asked.

"Leprosy! It's a disease that nobody gets any more. Certainly not around here," their mother assured them. "Let's not hear any more on that subject."

Kathleen always felt better, turning into her own driveway, having arrived safely home. There was no sign of Flakey Ferguson. Good. Yet terrible things were happening everywhere. At least, for today, they had not happened to her or the children. Just yesterday, she had been on the phone with her sister Grace.

"You remember Burris from Ninth Street?"

"Isn't he the one who drank?"

"Now he's gone and done it."

"What did he do?"

"Driving that old heap of his, drunk as a skunk. He ran right into a Stick-EE Buns delivery truck. Killed the driver."

Kathleen gasped.

"And that Stick-EE Buns driver was the sole support of a child with Downs."

"My Lord." Kathleen sighed. "No place is safe anymore."

That child. What would become of it? Put away, probably. A charity case for the rest of its life. Imagine what it would be like, having such a child. Both of her pregnancies had not been happy times; she was so afraid for both children.

If such a thing happened, Larry would not let her keep the baby. He'd have it sent from the hospital to an institution. He'd lie to everyone, saying their baby died. But their children were all right, and there was no way she would agree to going through another ordeal.

"Remember," Kathleen told the children as they ran into the house, "homework before electronics."

"Yes, Mom."

The mail was in the box. Most of it went into the recycle bin. She kept the electric bill and the newsletter from St. Catherine's Roman Catholic Church.

"Why do you read that?" Bobby once asked her. "We never go there."

"Because I have to see if anyone I know is mentioned."

"Who could you possibly know in a joint like that?"

Kathleen said nothing. This was a matter that she would not discuss with her children.

She sat down on the sofa, pulled off her shoes, and reminded herself not to worry so much. "What did I think, that the ugly thing was going to jump on her broom and chase me home?" Yet there was plenty more to worry about.

Larry, for instance. She always worried about her husband. *That he'd get caught.*

One of the worst nightmares she had was that Larry got into trouble and was going to be disbarred. Then some snoopy reporter found out he'd never even been admitted to the bar. Larry ended up in prison.

She'd have to sell this house and move with the children to a far less desirable neighborhood. Since she could no longer afford Greenleaf School, the kids would have to enroll in a chaotic public school where they would learn nothing. Each day, they would come home in tears, bullied by other children who knew their father was in the Big House. "Your daddy makes my daddy's license plates! Nyah, nyah, nyah!"

But it was only a silly dream.

Larry was so affable. He always had been. He was the sort who knew the right people. No matter what your problem was, you could just take it to good old Larry. He'd solve it for you. Did you have a parking ticket? A tax audit? You could always rely on Larry Kavanaugh; thus, no one looked too closely at him. He said he was an attorney; therefore, he must be one. Kathleen had been so charmed by him right from the start. That he had asked to marry her, when he had his pick of pretty girls, astounded her. Of course, she said yes.

However, her mother hated his guts.

"Larry Kavanaugh is nothing more than a manikin in an expensive suit," Mother tried to warn Kathleen. "He's a braggart and a liar. Nothing he says really ever checks out, does it? Well? Does it?"

"Of course it does, Mother. You just …"

"Remember when he said he was the quarterback at Jesuit High? Like he'd never stop bragging about it? I found out Mr. Touchdown never even made the team."

"Mother!"

"You know what else he did, just to get sympathy and attention for himself? He said his sister Carol was having such a hard time on chemotherapy. The truth is she never had cancer at all and got mad when she found out what he was saying about her. Carol was between jobs. All she needed was a rumor like that going around! That's why they're no longer speaking."

"Stop! I don't need to hear any more."

"You had better hear it now, young lady, before you say, 'I do.' There is a pattern developing here. Larry Kavanaugh is not that interested in you. He does not love you. He cannot. He's in love with Larry Kavanaugh. You're just going to be an accessory to Larry Kavanaugh. His acceptable wife. His cheering section who tells him how terrific he is no matter what he does. No matter whom he hurts. And when that person is you …"

"I won't hear any more of this! I love him!"

"How nice. You are both in love with the same person. Mark my words: with him, everything comes back to himself. Something goes right, and watch him grab all the credit for it. Something goes wrong, and someone else is to blame. I hope and pray you see through him before it's too late. As for myself, I'll be pleased to see the back of him."

Even then, Grace and Larry were cool to each other. Grace had given her a gift of kitchen implements and a promise.

"If this does not work out, remember I've got your back."

Mother was so bitter about the wedding that one night Kathleen and Larry eloped. Mother screamed, fainted, and took to her bed when she found out.

"Remember—when you come to your right mind, I will help you get this disaster annulled." Mother sighed. "And whatever you do, don't have any babies. He'll use them as a ball and chain to tie you to him."

"Mother, I'm sorry you feel that way," Kathleen replied, then turned around and left. She twisted the gold band on her finger. It felt strange and new there. Within a few months, Mother had a coronary and dropped dead in the supermarket. Kathleen and Larry were conspicuously absent from her wake and funeral.

Kathleen needed an aspirin. She swallowed it with a gulp of water and tried to banish thoughts of Mother from her mind. In a sense, it was a pity that Mother had not lived to see that their marriage was a success.

"Yes, indeed," Kathleen reminded herself, twisting her wedding ring again. It was a nervous habit of hers. "A smashing success, as long as I remember Larry Kavanaugh is always right, and anyone who disagrees with him is always wrong."

She turned on CNN. There was a prominent New York attorney being paraded down Fifth Avenue, surrounded by federal agents. Larry claimed to know him and had often dropped his name to those he was trying to impress.

CNN was not running the audio portion, but Kathleen could tell he was using the vilest language possible. Not the sort she would want the children to hear or repeat. A chill ran through her as she turned it off.

He got caught.

What are you looking at, toots?

I am afraid.

I'm so afraid that all of this is going to fall apart.

5

Scorch was the best. If ever a demon deserved gratitude, Scorch did. On a certain level, Satan must have known it too, because he had his own limitations. He may have been Lord of the Flies, Prince of the Air, blah blah, but he was not technically inclined. And he could not run Hell without Scorch. And he knew it.

Every once in a while, the walls of Hell rang with "Scorch! Get in here! Now!" The damned souls all knew Satan's laptop had malfunctioned again. Scorch went to work, then told Satan, "Problem solved. Click on the thumbscrew icon. See what happens?"

Satan would reply with a grunt. Or sometimes, "That's better." But did Scorch get any thanks? Certainly not. What Satan did not realize was that Scorch resented it, just as much as Roach resented his absence from *The Divine Comedy*. For which reason, Scorch was using his talents to aid and abet Roach's escape.

It took some effort, but Scorch was able to hack into the database of a popular chain store. There was a wealth of identities and credit card numbers, ripe for the picking. At that point, things in the Upper World improved for Roach. His default identity became Johnny LaRoche. He also had a large selection of other persons he could become, plus a never-ending line of credit. He obtained driver's licenses and passports for the human forms he was taking on. Paying for whatever Roach bought was someone else's problem. *Thank you, Scorch! You are a pal!*

Scorch also snuck tools out of Hell for Roach's use. There was a set of elixirs for each of the seven deadly sins. "Be careful with this one," Scorch said, holding up the beaker labeled Lust. "A little bit goes a long way."

There was also Scorch's connector. This was an ancient weapon used by demons, which Scorch had updated. A demon threw it at the back of a victim's head, and it created a tunnel, though which the demon had access to the victim's memories. It was nothing near possession but highly useful.

"For now, I can only spare you one of these babies, so be careful who you throw it at."

"You bet."

Roach was becoming more comfortable in a visible human form. The sore on his nose had gone down so much it was easy to conceal with makeup. With so much free money at his disposal, he took an apartment in a rather posh complex as his den and bought himself a car. His life was getting downright sweet.

Of course, there were places he needed to avoid. Libraries and bookstores, for instance, because just the sight of *The Divine Comedy* in any edition sent him into a rage. According to Scorch, he needed to avoid sacred places until he was more accustomed to the Upper World.

"Don't go near churches, mosques, or temples unless you know what you're doing. They're full of spirits you don't want to be near."

Roach understood. The thought of meeting up with Michael still gave him the willies. But they also attracted demons. If a bounty hunter cornered him, the sweet life was over.

"Be very careful around Catholic priests. All of them are certified exorcists. At least, they learn it in school. But you know, Roach, how much difference there is between a classroom and the real thing."

"I know it, all right!" He still got the shivers when he remembered speaking with other demons who had been successfully exorcised. *There is a weapon used in the Upper World. The still-living call it a Taser. And that's what it is like. They Tase you, over and over again. They wear you down. And then they grab you by your gizzard and heave you back into Hell!*

"See, they all memorize the procedure, but they don't have any experience. They're all talk. Can't do a thing to you. But if you get one who has done this sort of thing before, you can end up as roadkill. Be careful who you mess with!"

"I sure will," Roach promised.

"Another thing you need to avoid. Kids. And animals. A lot of them can see right through you."

"I hear you."

"Just know what you're doing is all I'm saying," Scorch advised him. "Think of some places as the big time."

Other things were so big-time that Roach felt it best to avoid them for now. The idea of trying a full possession on a live human was one of them. Possession took time and patience, which Roach often lacked. It was best left to more senior demons. Too much could go wrong.

Roach felt himself getting better at passing himself off as human. One needed money to survive in the Upper World. Now that Roach had such a generous cash flow, he could pass himself off as a better class of still-living. Yet this better class was no different from the losers on the bottom. They were just as foolish and gullible. Only they worshipped money. The more money Roach flashed around, the more he was respected. And trusted.

Roach felt no obligation to become a gentleman of leisure. Paid work was not beneath his dignity, provided it brought misery to someone else. At one point, he'd taken the form of a woman and danced around a pole at the Pink Pussycat Lounge. An enticing neon sign flashed: Live! Nude! Fools stuffed his garter with large bills. But he got tired of that and moved on to better things. Lust was the easiest of the seven deadly sins. There were better things: so many internet swindles. He sat on the boards of several fake charities. Cash just kept pouring in.

Then there were his hobbies. He met a thirteen-year-old girl online and sent her a picture of a wholesome teen boy, saying it was him. In a sense, he liked her, because her parents thought of her as a little princess. They spoiled her rotten. Her name was Eden. It fit well. Gullible as Eve but as mean as the snake. To Roach, she bragged about her shoplifting adventures at the mall. Mommy and Daddy never seemed to wonder about where she got so many expensive things. She totally enjoyed cyberbullying girls in her class whom she called Shamu, Tin Grin, and Pizza Face.

Yes, Roach saw her potential, but she wasn't worth the effort it would take to possess her. Instead, it would be more fun to teach her a lesson she'd never forget. First, he said he was in love with her and wanted to be her boyfriend. She eagerly agreed. Roach asked that as a pledge of her love for him, she needed to send him some naked selfies.

"Gee, I don't know," Eden replied. "Isn't that dangerous? I'd just die if somebody else sees them."

"Darling, this is a symbol of our sacred love. I could not stand to let anyone else see them!"

"Well, all right."

Roach was aware that there was a thin line between art and pornography. The pictures Eden sent were nowhere near art. This little stinker did not have any sense at all. He forwarded everything to Scorch. The following day, the images appeared anonymously in the phones of several classmates, all her teachers, her principal, the superintendent of schools, and, of course, Mommy and Daddy.

What a riot that was! But enough for now. One had to get back to work and keep the cash flow gushing.

Roach took on the form of a deposed Nigerian prince who needed to transfer several million dollars and forwarded an email to those on Scorch's sucker list. Life in the Upper World could be beautiful. Roach should have gone rogue long ago.

6

Kathleen's insomnia had gotten a lot worse. She had been trying for hours to get to sleep as Larry snored beside her. She looked at the digital clock. Three in the morning. No, this was not going to work.

Kathleen Kavanaugh did not believe in sleeping pills. They were only another symptom of moral weakness. She got up, put on her robe, and checked on the kids. Jeanine looked so innocent. Kathleen bent down and kissed her forehead. Bobby had tossed off his Transformers cover, so Kathleen put it back over him before going downstairs.

Everything was just as she left it, the living room tidied up, the dinner dishes done. The house was not on fire. ISIS fighters were not raiding the fridge. Why was this happening to her? Lately, she felt more fearful and apprehensive than ever.

If only she could talk to Grace. What kept her sister away from her? It was true, Grace could be snide, but Larry was downright nasty on the topic of Grace.

"She's never been married, no boyfriend either," Larry sneered. "Just her damn cats. What does that tell you?"

"It tells me that Grace loves cats. And that she's happy as she is. Larry, she's a registered nurse in the ER at St. Luke's. Big responsibility."

Larry made a face. He got ugly when Grace was around. At least he did not have a problem when Kathleen and Grace got together on their own. He assumed that Grace wanted their marriage to fail and was circling like a vulture above it.

Well, if their marriage did go down the tubes, it would not be due to Grace. There were so many other things to worry about.

For example, today. The children were watching the original *King*

Kong, which was one of their favorites. Bobby thought the airplanes were a scream. But it reminded her of a situation she did not want to think about. It was the same one the children must never know. Bobby could tell she was unnerved.

"Don't be alarmed, Mom," Bobby tried to comfort her. "Those chains are made of chrome steel."

Kathleen tousled his hair and called him the best little boy ever. But she could not stay to see the rest of the film.

"What is your problem? Why are you so fidgety? Have you been talking to Goofy Grace again? She tell you anything else to brighten up your day?" Larry asked her at dinner.

"No ... no ..."

"You have got to stop this, Kathleen. It's not good for you. Besides, nothing bad is going to happen."

"Larry, how can you know that?"

"Look," he began, "I've taken steps to ..." He seemed to be searching for the right words.

"Okay, I've taken steps to make sure that nothing really bad happens. To me, you, or the kids. It's kind of like, well, an insurance policy."

"You bought us an insurance policy? What kind?"

"Well ... it's not really that ..."

"Then what is it? May I at least look over the policy? Who sold it to you? And how much is this costing?"

"Honey, it's not really like that. All it means is you are wasting your time whenever you worry. So, drop it. You will be safe no matter what happens. Have a little faith in me. Believe me."

Kathleen had been through enough with Larry to know that when he said, "Believe me," things went terribly wrong. She looked out the window. There was no traffic at this hour, no lights on, not even in Flakey's house. Kathleen waited to make sure that all was silent, no one else was awake in this house. Then she went into the den and opened up Larry's rolltop desk.

Strange, it was just a bit chillier in here than it was in the living room. She hoped it was nothing big. If there was a problem with the furnace, Larry would put the repair off as long as possible, then whine about what it cost.

Again, everything else that was there before was still in place. The checkbook. Old tax returns. Insurance on their house and cars. Absolutely nothing that looked like a new policy.

"I wish I knew what was going on." She sighed, then went back to the living room. She had read all the magazines on the table and really should toss them into the recycle bin. But there was the newsletter from St. Catherine's, which she had not read yet.

Certainly, the Kavanaughs were not religious. Kathleen and Larry had both been raised Catholic but drifted away in college. Once they were married outside the church, they both decided that was it. No going back. As for the children, they were not baptized. Let them decide what they wanted to do when they grew up. As Bobby said, "You don't know anybody there, nobody there knows you, and so what's the big deal here?"

St. Catherine's was where they would go to Mass, if they ever did, which they did not. It was an affluent suburban parish made up of souls like Kathleen and Larry: Irish, from modest backgrounds, who had gone upwardly mobile quickly. There were many now in St. Catherine's who had gone to elementary school with Kathleen. And there was the problem. Bobby did not understand that there were many who might know her—and that terrible event.

Kathleen combed through the newsletter, looking for names. Just names. And there was the picture and name she feared the most: Dorothy Marie Walsh. *If you are interested in a trip to Washington next January for the March for Life, call Dorothy.*

The years had not been kind to Dorothy's face, but she still had that pitying grin on her face, seeming to say, "You poor wretch!" That had not changed since they were both children.

Kathleen trembled. The letter did not say anything more about Dorothy. But at least she had something to keep her busy. And perhaps, with luck, next January she'd take her plastic fetus and parade into another blizzard, then freeze.

Dorothy knew of the thing that had happened to Kathleen's family when they were both in second grade. Something that Kathleen had never disclosed, not even to Larry. Had he known, he might not have been so eager to marry her. And of course her children were never going to find out about it. But Dorothy knew. And Dorothy had the memory of an elephant.

Even in kindergarten, Dorothy was in training to be the class Mean Girl. The nuns tolerated her because she had a beautiful singing voice and did solos with the choir. This went right to her head.

"My mommy says she hopes Jimmy rots in jail forever," Dorothy had told her in class, before Sister Rosa reprimanded her. That didn't stop Dorothy: "My mommy says your big brother is a monster."

Kathleen was shaking now, bent over on the ottoman. Her brother Jimmy had never, as they said, "been right." She had no memory of ever loving him. All she felt around him was fear. Some joked that "his biceps is bigger than his brain." Children, especially, could be so cruel. Jimmy did not attend school; he never learned to read and write. Kathleen asked her mother many times if Jimmy could go live somewhere else. But Mother felt it was a sin to "put him away."

Jimmy was not supposed to leave the house by himself. Once he turned twelve, he got restless and much harder to control. Jimmy frightened so many of the neighbors, they called the police when they saw him wandering alone during the day. He vandalized mailboxes, broke into cars, and honked their horns. He became angry at a pack of boys who chanted "El Retardo" at him and chased them for several blocks. Still, Mother could not bring herself to send him away, even though she was being ostracized for it.

Finally, at sixteen, Jimmy snuck out at night, got on a city bus, and got off in a distant part of town. There, he started shouting racial slurs. A fight broke out. By the time the police broke it up, another young man was dead on the sidewalk, his skull split open by Jimmy.

Jimmy was arrested. It was on the local TV news, in all the papers. The shame was unbearable. Jimmy was found to be not responsible for his actions and put into a hospital for the violently insane.

Mother went to see Jimmy every Sunday. Once she died, Kathleen abandoned him. She did not know if Grace also cut him off, nor did she care to know.

The nuns at school were careful to be protective of Kathleen and Grace, but Dorothy always found a way to say hurtful things to them. "My mommy says that when you have babies, they'll be crazy too."

Dorothy was so vitriolic that Mother Superior ordered her parents to put her in another school. It was a relief to see her gone.

And she had the good sense to stay gone. At least until after Kathleen had Jeanine and was pushing her stroller through a downtown park on a pleasant spring day. She heard someone call her name and couldn't quite place the voice. She turned around and was horrified to see Dorothy's distinctive grin.

"I thought so! Kathleen McGrath! Mercy, how long has it been?"

Kathleen was too shocked say anything.

"Why, I was just thinking about you! I remember, a while ago, didn't I hear something about your getting married? And to Larry Kavanaugh? Well, I guess someone had to marry him, sooner or later!"

She laughed at her own joke. "And look at this. A baby girl. What an adorable little face. She's going to look just like you! Well, I must be running along, but it was great seeing you. Give my regards to Larry. He's a lucky guy!"

And with that, she was gone. Kathleen stood still awhile, then pushed the stroller quickly back home, ran into the powder room, and threw up.

As a rule, she did not believe in prayer. But she prayed that she'd never encounter Dorothy again. Her prayer went unanswered.

It was at least five years later. Kathleen was at the mall. By then, she'd had Bobby and was waiting in line with both the children to see Santa Claus. Bobby was a toddler, but Jeanine was old enough to have made a list of everything she wanted.

"Why, as I live and breathe! Isn't it Kathleen, who married Larry Kavanaugh?"

Oh no! Not here, not again!

"Look at you! Don't you look terrific! That coat is so becoming on you. And a little boy this time? Oh, let me see him!"

Kathleen pulled Bobby a step back. She wanted to call mall security but was afraid of making a scene.

"Well, whatever. Maybe I was wrong about Larry. You seem to be doing all right. And such beautiful children, you must be so proud. But tell me ..." Dorothy dropped her voice. "Do they know? I mean, it would be a terrible thing if they found out by accident."

27

Kathleen felt her blood congeal. At that moment, Santa let out a "Ho! Ho! Ho!" and held out his arms to welcome Jeanine.

"Excuse me," Kathleen said and turned away. She assisted Jeanine into Santa's lap and gave her the wish list. When she looked up, Dorothy was gone.

Do they know? I mean, it would be a terrible thing if they found out by accident.

Not even a Mafia capo could make a clearer threat. Kathleen had one memento of the occasion, a picture taken by an elf, of Jeanine talking to Santa, while her mother looked ready to drop.

Since then, she had not seen Dorothy, except in her nightmares. In these nightmares, Dorothy wanted money. *More and more money, or I tell those kids the truth.* The more Jeanine grew, the more she was in the vulnerable position of looking like her mother. Anyone who knew Kathleen McGrath in second grade could take one look at Jeanine and swear she was the exact same child. But only Dorothy had come right out with that threat.

Kathleen sank into a light sleep on the ottoman. She was still aware of being in the living room, but her mind was drifting. Dorothy had gotten so demanding Kathleen could not pay her what she wanted. Not without Larry's finding out. So, one day, when Dorothy saw Jeanine at the playground, she grabbed her and stuffed her into the car.

"Your mommy says it's all right for me to take you on a trip." Dorothy grinned. "No, she won't be mad!"

Dorothy took her to that mental hospital, into the back ward where Jimmy was. "Here is your uncle Jimmy, the one you never met! See how big he is? Did you know he killed a man with his bare hands? Want to give him a big hug and a kiss?"

Kathleen's mind cried out to her daughter: *Throw your arms across your eyes and scream, Jeanine! Scream for your life!*

The terrified child let out a blood-curdling scream that dissolved into the sound of an alarm clock ringing from upstairs. Kathleen was jolted awake. Larry got out of bed and called, "Kathleen? Where are you?"

"Down here. I'm just getting an early start on breakfast."

"That's nice."

Indeed, it was. The sky was getting lighter outside. Another day had begun, and her family did not know about Jimmy. They did not know that she'd pay Dorothy Walsh any amount, just to keep her big mouth shut.

Thus far, she was safe, and that was all that mattered.

7

Roach assumed his default human form of Johnny LaRoche and went for a stroll near St. Catherine's Church. He would not dare go inside. But it was a delightful day. So many were out enjoying it, and Roach was wondering whose life he could ruin next.

He saw an old man feeding pigeons and sent him a thought: *Your son never calls, because he hates your guts.* He glanced into a passing stroller, and the baby woke abruptly and let out a wail. He felt his phone vibrate.

ScorchIT@inferno.org: roach that you?

Roach@hellraiser.com: yo

ScorchIT@inferno.org: wazzup

Roach@hellraiser.com: Life sweeter every day. How the hell's Hell?

ScorchIT@inferno.org: hotter

Roach@hellraiser.com: WTH?

ScorchIT@inferno.org: Satan's a lot madder. Upped the price on your head. Found out some of the stuff you did.

Roach@hellraiser.com: LOL

ScorchIT@inferno.org: I'm serious bro remember Eden?

Roach@hellraiser.com: woo woo little hottie! what about her?

ScorchIT@inferno.org: tried to kill self. drank furniture polish.

Roach@hellraiser.com: too damn bad she dead yet?

ScorchIT@inferno.org: mommy & daddy got her to ER on time still in ICU really bad shape

Roach@hellraiser.com: my heart just bleeds meanest damn teen queen in Herbert Hoover Junior High

ScorchIT@inferno.org: when Satan found out started getting jealous you beating him at his own game & he don't like it

Roach@hellraiser.com: that's tough thanks for heads up

ScorchIT@inferno.org: watch your back bro

Roach replaced his phone, then heard a growling sound. A very small dog had come up to him and started to yap loudly.

"Get lost, you dumb mutt," Roach told him. He kept on yapping, then grabbed Roach's pants leg and pulled. Roach cursed and tried to kick him off, but the dog ripped off part of the fabric and ran away.

"Shit! My good pants, ruined!" The dog ran so fast that he was now out of the range in which Roach could harm him.

"Oh, I'm so sorry!" a woman said. She was wearing a religious medal, which Roach found distasteful, as was her pitying grin. "He didn't bite you, did he? Did he break the skin?" Then Roach saw a thin line of blood running down.

"Son of a bitch, yes!"

"Mercy, some of these people who let their dogs run loose ought to be ashamed of themselves. He was wearing a collar. He must belong to someone. We'll have to find out who owns him, to see if he's rabid."

"To see if he's …"

"Because if he tests positive for rabies, you will need to start getting shots. So really, you should call your doctor right away."

Roach threw back his head and roared with laughter. *Stupid woman, since when does a demon catch rabies?*

"Well!" she said, backing away, thinking that he was quite possibly mad. "I was merely trying to be of assistance. And you, young man, it might help if you cleaned up your vocabulary. This is a public place. Ladies and children are present."

She walked off in a huff. With her back turned to him, Roach was able to throw Scorch's connector at the back of her head. Direct hit! Now he could access the database in her mind. She might be useful.

She'd be sorry she ever showed pity to the great Roach.

8

Kathleen's anxiety seemed to be getting worse. And Larry, of course, was of no help.

Here was another sleepless night. Well, only partially, because she'd had a nightmare and woke up with a gasp, which woke Larry.

"What's the matter now?" he grumbled.

"I was at the traffic light with the kids in the back seat. That woman at the bus stop opened her mouth, and this forked tongue shot out and wrapped around Jeanine."

"You're not making any sense. Besides, I have to be up at six. And I need my sleep."

Thus saying, he rolled over and was snoring again. Kathleen got out of bed and went back downstairs. She thought about her mother.

In that brief interval between their wedding and her mother's sudden death, Mother asked, "And are you happy with him?"

"Of course, I am!" she insisted.

"All right! Far be it from me to criticize!"

No. She was no longer happy with Larry. Why, then, did she agree to this marriage?

So many things Larry did hurt her. The way he kept snipping at Grace was one of them. At one point, he had started a rumor that Grace stayed single because she was a lesbian.

The rumor got around to Grace. One day, he found her and Kathleen on the porch laughing about it. "Don't you think that if it were the least bit true, I would have come out of the closet long ago?" Grace asked. Then she gave Larry a dirty look. "I wonder where that story came from. Hmmmm?"

"I have no idea," Larry replied.

Kathleen often wondered if Grace was lonely. Or missed not having a child of her own. Or afraid, living alone, with only two cats for company. She did not seem so. Kathleen wondered if she could change her life for Grace's. It was too late now; that much was certain.

She asked herself, did she really love Larry? Or was the real reason that she was afraid of Jimmy?

Yes. I am still afraid of him.

She wondered if Jimmy could escape and come looking for her. Unlike Grace, she could not live on her own. With Larry, she felt safe.

At least she did for the first year or so. It took her that long to realize that Lawrence Paul Kavanaugh Jr. was no Prince Charming.

Having any children at all was an issue. She was so terrified of giving birth to another Jimmy. Her entire family had been so vague that she could not know if there was a pattern of mental disability in her DNA. But Larry insisted on children and thought her anxiety attacks during her pregnancies were normal.

Kathleen had reason to wonder: did Larry really want children? Or a wallet full of pictures of children?

Although neither child showed any sort of defect, she had them both tested. The results surprised her.

"In fact, you really do have a pair of special-needs children here," the doctor said. "These two are gifted like you would not believe! I'd say congratulations on both, but they're a big responsibility."

Responsibility was not Larry's favorite word.

"With the proper education, there's no limit to what they can accomplish. I'd recommend a school with a STEM program."

"STEM?" Kathleen asked.

"Science, technology, engineering, and math. If they were my kids, I'd say Greenleaf. Greenleaf is especially good at getting girls interested in science. Now Greenleaf isn't cheap by any means, but I don't want to see Jeanine discouraged. Think about it."

Larry thought about it. He was not pleased. "I thought I wouldn't have to pay any tuition till they got to college," he mumbled. "They'd better pay me back when they get their Nobel Prizes."

"Oh, Larry!" she said. The pattern was getting clearer as their marriage went on. Larry Kavanaugh was all about Larry Kavanaugh.

Plus he was in no danger of being Father of the Year. He never attended a meeting or event at Greenleaf. Not once did he sign their report cards. "Too busy, too tired." It was said that if he ever went to Greenleaf, he'd get lost in the corridors.

Lately he had been crabbing about Bobby's inventions and experiments. "Boy won't be happy till he blows the whole house up." If the children were disappointed in him, they knew better than to show it.

It seemed he never spoke directly to them in an indoor voice. He was always yelling.

"Stay out of my den!"

"Don't touch that!"

"Turn that racket down!"

"No, you can't have your friends over here. They might break something!"

"No, you can't have a puppy or a kitty!"

"No, no, no!"

At least, when they visited Grace, they could play with her cats. But that was all.

Kathleen thought of that time when Larry had taken them both to the playground in the park as toddlers. They both came back wailing. Bobby had such a large hematoma that Kathleen rushed him to the ER at St. Luke's. By chance, Grace was on duty.

"What happened here?" the doctor asked.

"Um, he was swinging real high, and he fell," Larry muttered.

"You were supposed to be watching him!" Kathleen snapped.

Bobby recovered from his injury, but Larry never did recover from the dirty look Grace shot him.

But had there been a change? Did he mean it when he said he'd done something to provide them with a secure future? What, then? Why wouldn't he say anything more about it? As his wife, shouldn't she have the right to know? Didn't she have to sign something?

Another worry: Larry might have forged her signature onto some sort of legal document. If he did, it would not be the first time.

Kathleen went into the den and opened up the rolltop desk. Again, no change in the important papers section. There was still that locked metal box in the bottom drawer. There were other drawers here, plus Larry's file cabinet, so full of unpleasant memories.

When they married, Larry had been a furniture salesman at Logan's. He was making a good income and doing well. Larry could accomplish so much with superficial charm and fake caring about his customers. He would tell them, "Of course you want Danish modern—perfect for your new house." Then he'd come home to Kathleen and say, "Danish modern in a center hall colonial? They have a lot more money than sense."

Then he and a fellow salesman, Rick Davis, had an idea. They would become entrepreneurs as founders of Miracle Furniture. So, they quit their jobs and set out on their own, with Rick owning 51 percent, Larry 49 percent. Their capital was far from adequate. Larry decided to secure a second trust on their home. Kathleen was not pleased with the notion and outraged when she learned that Larry had forged her signature on the loan application.

"How could you do this to me?" she demanded.

"Honey, come on! Don't you realize how rich we're going to get? In no time, we're going to sell this place and buy one of those estates in Swan Pointe. We'll have a swimming pool out back. In no time, we'll be entertaining all the elites."

"You are a fool! You'd fall for anything!" They did not speak for weeks after that.

The grand opening of their store bombed. It snowed. Hardly anyone showed up, and those who did didn't buy anything. The building was ugly, and its location could not be seen from the main drag. The parking lot was inadequate.

Larry was overwhelmed with responsibilities. He was supposed to hire salespeople and deliverymen and had no idea how to do these things. Larry did not think to check references. His sales staff was unreliable, and the deliverymen were often drunk. He became a deer in the headlights of an approaching car, too terrified to move.

A riddle went around as to how Miracle Furniture got its name: if your sofa gets delivered on time and is not smashed to smithereens, it's a miracle.

The business did not even last a year. He and Rick, who had been such good friends, became sworn enemies. To Larry's mind, the whole fiasco was clearly Rick Davis's fault.

Those files had never been thrown out. The memory was bitter, and the sad thing was, to this day, they were still making payments on that mistake. At least Larry found another job that did not involve putting him in a position of leadership. Larry had what he needed: a manager who told him what to do and how to do it.

His job in the Transit Authority allowed for an adequate lifestyle. He could say he was an attorney. He could say he was the King of Glory if he so desired. No one cared. But their losses were never recouped. And no one could ever remind Larry of Miracle Furniture without having him blow up.

Kathleen continued her search in the file drawer. Perhaps whatever Larry had bought them was hidden in here. No, nothing looked recent. All four drawers yielded nothing.

"Another waste of time," Kathleen decided. She sat down at the desk and perused the checkbook. Everything looked current: mortgages, utilities, car payments, Greenleaf tuition. As always, not much was left over. Yet something still felt wrong. She read over the checking log for the past six months, in search of a large payment to some person or place she did not know. That yielded nothing.

She had been forced to admit to herself, many times, Larry was a cheapskate. He was always complaining about what everything cost. During that time when Miracle Furniture was circling the drain, he continuously whined about how much advertising cost. If she asked him, "Can't you buy a spot on the radio? A page in the paper?" he always said, "No, no, too expensive." And just look at what happened.

One thing she was sure of: if she had to start withdrawing funds from their joint accounts, without his knowledge, he'd waste no time in finding out about it. And he would demand an explanation.

"Who in the hell is this Dorothy M. Walsh? And what are we paying her for?"

Kathleen put her head down on the desk and cried.

9

Roach got back to his den and tore off his pants in a rage. He'd never wear this pair again. And indeed, that mangy cur bit out quite a chunk of his leg. Roach quickly changed his form to a similar better-looking man, but a scar still showed.

"Dammit!" he shouted. But at least, on his lower leg, he could keep it covered. No one needed to see it or question how it got there.

Roach pulled on another pair of pants. He was still furious. But he knew enough not to act right away.

The connector was a weapon used by demons since Adam and Eve's expulsion from Eden. Scorch had improved it. As a rule, Roach dreaded the lectures demons were required to attend in the Hitler aula. Sometimes, demons being demons, a good fight broke out in the stands, or Satan lost his temper. However, Scorch's technical presentations were kind of interesting.

The original connector was a tunnel from a demon's mind directly into the mind of one victim. Most victims had not known it was there; a few became aware and could get rid of it before Scorch's latest upgrade.

"One connector can now infest multiple victims. Think of a computer virus," Scorch explained. "Now, the virus is sent through the connector into a human mind, and once there, it copies itself to everyone the victim has ever known. Any questions thus far?"

Orcus had to know: "Every single person, even the slightest acquaintance?"

"Well, yes and no," Scorch said. "If it's a casual or passing acquaintance, the copy is likely to be too weak to be of use to us. But it will be there. Now let's posit there is a strong bond between your primary and secondary victim."

Orcus groaned. "Not love, not again! No more flowers and candy!"

"No, not at all, and here is the real beauty of this system! The connection has to be hate-based."

"Now you're talking!"

"If your victim hates someone, or is jealous or resentful, or fantasizes about bringing harm to someone else, the copy will be flawless. And my new and improved connector will give you the exact same access to the mind of your secondary victim. This includes, as a bonus, the ability to enter the secondary's dwelling place without his knowledge or consent."

"Just like we've always done with primary victims?"

"You got it!"

A cheer went up. Demons had never been able to enter a home without being asked inside. Now, all of that was going to change.

Roach had only been able to get one connector from Scorch. He had thrown it in a state of rage. He only hoped that, in his anger, he had not wasted it on another nobody like Larry Kavanaugh.

He'd find out soon enough. It was best to access the connector for the first time while the victim was sleeping. Indeed, everything was always best in the dark. To make sure his victim was receptive, Roach waited till midnight. In the meantime, he watched a beauty contest on his flat-screen TV. Talent, swimsuit, and evening gown. Only one could win. The rest had to fake being happy for her.

Admit it, Roach thought to them. *You want to scratch her eyes out.* Their plastic grins stayed in place. What a bunch of idiots.

Then midnight struck. He relaxed himself before entering the tunnel the connector had made for him.

Then he drifted through the tunnel he created, like a spider through her web, in search of her prey. His journey took him to a modest but respectable part of the city.

There was a small brick house, surrounded by a hedge, with a vinyl garden trellis. The house itself could have been painted by Norman Rockwell. The front yard was way too full of plants. Roach neared the front door then jumped back.

Oh no! There was a statue of the Virgin Mary on the front porch. She was looking up to heaven and stepping on a snake. Roach found that revolting. He had to keep going. He owed it to Scorch not to waste this connector. Roach extended his head through the front door.

Heeere's Johnny!

The inside was worse. There were sticky-sweet pictures of Jesus, Mary, and St. Theresa of the Roses. There were even pictures of that horrible woman whom he'd met in the park. In one, she was bundled up, standing in the middle of Pennsylvania Avenue with a life-sized plastic fetus. In another, she was standing by a fountain in St. Peter's Square with that same treacly expression on her face.

"So far, so good," he said to himself, crawling the rest of the way in. "At least I know I have the right address."

What struck him as out of place was, in such a home, you might find benevolent spirits. You might even run into St. Theresa of the Roses. But here, there was nothing and no one.

Roach continued upstairs. Indeed, she was snoring lightly in a childish single bed. And there was not a soul in the house with her. Not even a cat or dog to give him any problems.

Roach studied her face. No question. This was the right one. It was time to begin. Time to ask the ritual question, which by coincidence began the dreaded process of exorcism.

"By some sign, tell me your name."

"Oh … are you talking to me?" she whispered back.

"Tell me your name," Roach said in his most authoritarian-exorcist tone.

"Dorothy Marie Walsh."

Roach paused as the connector gave him copies of her memories and began sending out the virus to her contacts.

"And who might you be?" she dared to ask.

"My name is not important. What is important, Dorothy, is that I care very much about you. And I want to see you happy and content. Are you, Dorothy? Is there anything you want that you do not have?"

"Are you my guardian angel?"

Roach felt another wave of revulsion. "Just tell me about yourself, who you are."

"I don't know," Dorothy replied. "They always told me in school to be careful. There are some evil things out there."

"Who told you that?"

"The nuns."

"Dorothy, please. That may be fine for a child to believe. Such nonsense keeps the little monsters in line. But surely you know by now that evil spirits don't really exist!"

"I suppose not. What can I say?"

"Say who and what you are."

"Well, you know my name. I've never been married, no children. I'm a consecrated virgin."

A virgin? No wonder. Roach found her to be so utterly repulsive. "Go on," he said. He had to go on prying till he found her weakest spot.

"I'm a member of St. Catherine's Church where I'm very active. Oh, and I sing in the choir, and I do solos too."

"Then you like to sing, Dorothy?"

"I am so good at it. Why, last Christmas, when I did 'O Holy Night,' there was not a dry eye in the entire church."

"You take great *pride* in your singing voice, don't you, Dorothy?"

"Oh, yes. I've been singing since I was a child, and I studied voice with—"

"Tell me one thing, Dorothy. Has anyone ever tried to interfere with your singing? Think all the way back now."

Dorothy sighed and said, "Yes."

"Who would do such a terrible thing?"

"There were two of them." Roach heard her teeth grinding. Now he was getting somewhere. Genuine hate. "The McGrath sisters."

"Who are they? What did they do?"

"Kathleen and Grace McGrath. Kathleen was in my second-grade First Communion class. Grace was in kindergarten at the time."

"Tell me what happened."

"They had a teenage brother. Jimmy. Something was wrong with him. With his mind. Big, strong fellow but mentally, very weak. Now, Mrs. McGrath did not want to put him away even though he was wandering around and causing problems. My mother, of course, forbade me to go over to the McGrath house. Much too dangerous. Mother said that Mrs. McGrath must have committed a terrible sin once and that Jimmy was her punishment. And a lot of people agreed with her."

"Why, that's a very wise observation," Roach encouraged her.

"I felt obliged to keep reminding Kathleen and Grace of that. It never bothered me to make them cry. I felt so good when they ran off in tears. And then Jimmy … one night he got out and ended up in another part of town. He confronted some other boys, called them an ugly name … a name in reference to their race. A fight broke out. Someone called the police. When they saw Jimmy pounding the head of one of those boys into the sidewalk, blood was everywhere. And that poor boy was already dead."

"Excuse me, Dorothy, but what has this got to do with your singing?"

"I'll get to that." Dorothy was enjoying this. "Jimmy was arrested. Of course, the McGraths could not keep him at home any longer. He was finally put away. There was an uproar for a while; you could not look at the news without hearing about it. At school, the nuns told us to be kind to the McGrath girls. I thought, please! I felt it was my place to keep reminding them of what Jimmy had done. And besides, it was almost time for the spring choir recital."

"And you had a part in that?"

"I was the star! It was going to be a scene in the sky, in the clouds. The other children would be dressed as candy bars. I already had my costume, a long pink gown with sequins and tiara, and I would sing …"

Dorothy gasped. Although sleeping, a tear ran down her cheek. "I would sing 'On the Good Ship Lollipop!' And do a dance too!"

Roach had to force himself to keep from laughing.

"Only … only … the nuns … the more they warned me to stop tormenting the McGrath sisters, the more I did it."

"Of course!" said Roach. "It was your Christian duty!"

"And then, one day I got called in to Mother Superior's office. My mother and father were there. She told them that I'd been so cruel to the McGraths I was being expelled. And that the recital was cancelled!" Dorothy sniffled. "What the McGraths put me through, oh, it was simply terrible! I was so humiliated. I wanted so many bad things to happen to them."

"Dearest Dorothy, you have my utmost sympathy. I certainly can understand what you went through!" Roach thought of his deliberate exclusion from *The Divine Comedy*. "Remember I am your friend. And I want what's best for you. Tell me—what became of the McGraths, do you know?"

"Grace, well, she became a nurse at St. Luke's, the last I heard. But Kathleen got married to Larry Kavanaugh."

"Wait! Wait! Who did you say?"

"She married Larry Kav—"

"Lawrence Paul Kavanaugh Jr.?"

"That's the one. He's an attorney."

"Ah!"

"You know him?"

"Let's say we've transacted some business together. But what do you know of him?"

"Not much. We were never close or anything; we just ran with the same crowd in college. I personally never dated him. But he was something of an odd bird."

"In what way?"

"He was such a chatterbox. Talk, talk, talk. Mostly about himself. Many thought it was a load of bull, well, I won't say that word. But he talked about other people too."

"What other people?"

"Rich, famous, successful people. Always claiming he was good friends with them or had some sort of connection to them. For instance, he said he knew a novelist, the one who wrote *Debacle in the Desert*. Said they were such good friends, that Larry was the inspiration for Marc. And then Larry said he was going to fly out to Hollywood to screen test for the role of Marc in the film. But nothing ever came of that. And as you know, Todd Oakwood played Marc."

"Certainly, everyone knows that," Roach assured her.

"Larry was a charming sort. That, I remember. Always the life of the party, provided the party was all about him. I was surprised to hear he'd married a killjoy like Kathleen McGrath."

"Did you see Kathleen or Larry since they got married? Think back."

"Yes, I did see Kathleen a few times. I tried to be pleasant with her, you know, trying to be big about it, in spite of all she had done. But I must say she was far from polite. Yes, very rude to me, right in front of her children. Fine example to set."

Roach thought back. Kavanaugh hadn't said anything about his family. Roach presumed he had one, as the contract was signed in the den of the house on Split Tree Circle. There were pictures of a woman (Kathleen?) and two children. But all Kavanaugh was interested in was a guarantee that he personally would not be caught in any illegal activity. *"Where do I sign?"*

Roach even reminded him, "What you sign here is final. You can't go back and amend this thing for something else you want in the future. You do not have more than one soul. This is it." Kavanaugh insisted this was all he wanted for himself. And signed, right on the dotted line. "I am of sound mind, and I execute this contract of my own free will. Lawrence Paul Kavanaugh Jr."

"I merely inquired," Dorothy chattered on.

"Excuse me. I was distracted," said Roach.

"When I last saw her, I only asked if her children knew about, well, their background."

"You mean about Uncle Jimmy, who hulked out and killed somebody?"

"If you care to put it that way. It's my belief that a child really should know these things rather than find out by accident later in life."

"And what did Kathleen say to you?"

"Nothing. So rude. I assume she's keeping it a secret from them. These things have a way of coming out."

"And, of course, the fact that Kathleen is keeping this secret puts her into a vulnerable position."

"How do you mean?"

"Suppose someone took it upon herself to disclose this information? Someone like you?"

"Why ... I never thought ..."

"Only you might refrain from telling them. Leave them in the dark. For a price."

"Oh my! Suppose she goes to the police? Isn't that illegal?"

"Not if you don't get caught. Kathleen is keeping a secret. Don't you think she is afraid? Dorothy, you have power over her. You can undo the wrong she did to you. You can claim what is rightfully yours."

Roach could see vast amounts of cash piling up in Dorothy's corrupt little soul. He had a flashback of Eve's hand reaching for the apple. "And you deserve so much more, Dorothy. Yes, much more. The world deserves to hear your beautiful voice. I can make all of that come true for you."

Roach reached out for the part of Dorothy that had gone dormant. He opened the Elixir of Lust vial. Scorch warned him that a little of this would go a long way. If that were true, a lot must be so much better.

He poured it into Dorothy's soul, then sent her an image of Larry Kavanaugh emerging naked from the shower. She made a squealing sound of delight. At that instant, the connector sent him a signal: 100 percent downloaded. The virus was fully distributed and functioning in everyone Dorothy hated.

"Go back to sleep now, Dorothy. Dream of Larry Kavanaugh, for he will dream of you. Lullaby, and good night ..."

Roach drifted back to his own den, collapsed on his bed, and heaved with laughter. This was better than his wildest imaginings!

10

The day had not gone well on Split Tree Circle. Larry woke up at six again, with his wife missing. He found her soon enough, sleeping with her head on his open rolltop desk. Drawers in his filing cabinet were hanging open.

"Kathleen!" he snapped. "What the hell do you think you are doing?"

She woke up with a start and a confused expression, touching the back of her head. There was a strange sort of headache there, one she had never felt before.

"These are my papers! My personal papers! Were you going through them?"

Kathleen glared at him. He did not notice the salt stains on her cheeks. "Your personal papers?" she asked him. "Last time I checked, I was your lawfully wedded wife. With all my worldly goods, I thee endow. Did that slip your mind?"

"I don't know what's gotten into you. But I want it stopped. This instant—do you hear me? Because if you don't …"

"Mom!" came from upstairs. "Jeanine's hogging the bathroom!"

"I am not!"

"Please excuse me," she said. "I have a far more urgent matter in need of my attention."

"You're excused. For now. I'm having breakfast at the diner. We will discuss this when I get home."

"I'm sure we will."

Kathleen pulled herself up the stairs, still touching the back of her head. Her dreams had been disturbing, but she could not recall them.

There was a bit about being touched where her hand was now by something that felt like it came out of a deep freeze.

Larry also ate his lunch and dinner at the diner. He wanted the kids to be in their own rooms, doing their homework, rather than have his big beef with Kathleen in front of them. They did not have to know. By the time he entered his own home, Lester Holt had said good night, and Kathleen was glaring at a blank TV screen.

"Kids upstairs?" he asked her.

"All of a sudden, you care about where they are? I am so impressed!"

"Don't do this, Kathleen. I've had a bad enough day. This has got to stop."

"Point well taken!"

"I want to know what's going on with you, why you prowl around this house like a stray cat in heat all night long."

"And I want to know what's going on. You said you … what? Did something? Bought some kind of insurance? Just in case something bad happens?"

"Look, I said nothing bad is going to happen. Because I'll always be able to take care of you. And the kids. Trust me on that one."

Kathleen threw her head back and laughed. "Oh, trust you? I'm supposed to trust you, and everything will be just peachy! When did I hear that song-and-dance act before?"

"Dammit, Kathleen, I've done more for you than you can ever know. So gimme a break, all right?"

"Trust you, because you know what you're doing! Oh, Larry, you're something else, you know? You ought to have your own TV show! Aren't you just a laugh a minute?"

"Dammit to Hell, will you quit nagging me?"

"And will you quit telling me to trust you? I trusted you before, Larry! Miracle Furniture! We were going to be millionaires! We'd live in a mansion in Swan Pointe! With a pool in the backyard! Thanks to you, we almost lost this house!"

"You know damn well that was not my fault! Davis screwed it up!"

Larry clenched his fists. His face turned bright red. Upstairs, Bobby's phone sent the secret signal to Jeanine's. "Woot! Woot! Woot!"

That meant abandon homework and hide under the bed. They both knew the drill.

"And will you at least tell me what you did? Sign some sort of contract? Shouldn't you have your own copy of it? Where is it? Why don't you want me to see it? Larry, I am your wife, and I have a right to know!"

"That does not mean you should."

"What have you gone and done? Are you somehow involved with … what? The Mafia? Some loan shark? I wouldn't put it past you, Larry. Do you realize the danger you've put us in?"

Larry picked Kathleen's mother's favorite vase off the mantelpiece and smashed it.

Kathleen collapsed onto the sofa, weeping. "Oh God, oh God, Larry! What have you gone and done!"

Larry sat down beside her. "Look—it's not what you think, honey. What will happen won't affect you or the kids at all. Just me, okay?"

"What have you done? Dear God, I'm your wife! Why can't you tell me what you've done?"

"Okay, I, um, Kathleen? I know, you might not even believe in this stuff, but, um, like, I sold my soul to the devil."

Kathleen said nothing.

"Honey, did you hear what I said?"

No response.

"Um, this means that nothing's gonna happen. Except of course when I die, which is a long way off, knock on wood." He tapped the coffee table. "Then I go straight to Hell. But that's then, and this is now. And in the meantime, I do and say what I want. And I won't get caught. Hey, um, you'll never see me headed for federal prison. Not like that poor schmuck in New York. Kathleen? Did you hear a word I said? Honey?"

Finally, she looked at him. "You sold. Your soul. To the devil."

"That's it, in a nutshell, yes."

"Did the devil give you a copy of whatever you signed?"

"No, sweetums, that's the thing. It was one of these duplicate forms. One goes in the file. That's in Hell. And the devil keeps the other in his personal file. That's how it's done. No triplicate forms."

"You dealt with the actual devil?"

"Well, no, honey, one of his demons."

"One of his demons. I see. Doesn't he have a whole bunch of them? Do we know which one?"

"Um, that's it. I can't recall his name. Sort of like an insect. Like you'd call an exterminator for. Stink Bug, I think."

"And did this Mr. Stink Bug give you his card?"

"No, he explained they don't use cards in Hell."

"Where did this take place?

"In the den. At my rolltop desk. While you were at the work and the kids were in school."

"And then I suppose Mr. Stink Bug vanished in a puff of smoke."

"No, he, um, he looked and acted like a normal guy."

"Oh. Mr. Stink Bug is just a normal guy, yes. Silly me, I thought you were mixed up with the Mafia."

"You are not, um, you're not mad, are you, honey?"

"Me? Mad? Oh, no, I'm not in the least bit mad."

"You still love me, don't you?" Larry asked in his most pitiful whine and reached out for her. "Can we kiss and then go upstairs and make up now? Aren't I your little bitty boy baby?"

Kathleen jumped up from the sofa. "You keep your filthy hands off of me!"

"Kathleen! Honey!"

"You either expect me to believe this incredible tale. Or you are nuts. Stark, raving nuts! You are crazy! And I don't want you near me or the children. Get out!"

"But—"

"You are crazy! You are crazier than Flakey Ferguson or ... or ..."

Kathleen did not finish her sentence. She could not speak of Jimmy. She ran upstairs into their bedroom and locked the door. "Get out of this house, you nutcase! Get out before I call the cops!"

"Honey! Darling!"

"Get out!"

Larry could not force the door open. He thought to run outside, get the extension ladder out of the garage, and use it to access the bedroom window. What he saw chilled his blood.

Kathleen had the window wide open. She was heaving out his socks and underwear. Then his casual clothing and pajamas. Then good suits and ties.

"You are a danger to yourself and others! I will not have you in my clean home! Go!"

She then heaved out his golf bag full of clubs. It landed with a resounding crash. Every other window on Split Tree Circle was lit up.

"All right, all right, I'll go. I'll be back in the morning and—"

"In the morning, I'm filing for a divorce. With a real, live lawyer. Not one like you, phony! Fake! Go!"

His toothbrush bounced off the sidewalk, as did his tube of Preparation H. Kathleen then slammed the window down. Larry picked them up with a few other essentials, stuffed them into his car, and drove away. Many pairs of eyes followed his taillights into the now-silent evening.

11

Roach had never been more pleased with himself. To think that this Dorothy, whom he had first found so repulsive, would turn out to be such a kindred soul. So much dry rot inside of her for him to work with! And Dorothy so naïve, she had no concept of what he really was.

However, he knew her. In all of her hate and jealousy and fear. All of her history. Can you believe, she was once a nun? Whoop-de-doo!

Roach also had a large volume of memory data from the connection with Kathleen, updated through yesterday morning. But this day called for a celebration. He felt he should go for a walk in the park. Yes, that park near the Kavanaugh house. He'd still be Johnny LaRoche in a different form. And he might even stroll by the Kavanaugh house, just to see what was going on.

Roach took care to stay far from children and animals. From the park, it should be easy to find Split Tree Circle. But he had forgotten just which way to go, and the GPS was not with him. He decided to come back on another day. Not important. He sat down on a park bench beside a tired-looking, middle-aged man.

Roach eyed him with contempt; another loser. He did not look well. Roach did a quick scan inside his body and saw why.

This fool has an aortic aneurism that could go ka-blooey at any minute. He's on borrowed time for sure.

Roach thought of an uproarious practical joke he could play on Satan. He'd find a way to kill off this fool. It ought to be easy. Then he'd snatch his soul, carry it into Hell, and storm into Satan's executive suite.

"Roach!" the ugly receptionist would shout. "Do you have an appointment?"

He'd ignore her. He'd walk right in while Satan was on the phone, chewing out a fellow demon. He'd heave the soul on to Satan's desk, spilling both in and out boxes, making a mess of all the paperwork involved in damnation. "Here's another dime a dozen, asshole!" he'd say and then leave, very quickly. It was worth a try.

"Pretty d-d-day, isn't it?" the stranger asked him.

"It'll do," Roach replied. *Can't talk right, either.*

"I c-come here lots of times," the loser said. "Mostly I st-stay home, but that's boring."

"You don't have to go to work?"

"N-no, I can't work. I got obsessive-compulsive dis-disorder real bad. Plus a wh-whole bunch of other stuff wrong with me. I'm on dis-disability."

Roach thought, *You won't be for long.* "You live around here?" he asked.

"Ye-yes, my house is close by. B-but it's not my house; it's my mother's. On-only she don't live with me no more. Mo-mother's in a nu-nursing home. She, she, she has Alz, Alz, Alzheimer's disease."

"I see. That's too bad."

"So, so, I live by, by myself in her house. It's a big house. I grew, grew up in it."

"That's nice." The aneurism looked stable for the time being. A good shock ought to send him over. How to do it, though, was a problem. He could not make his move in a public place. Unless he could do something to gain the fool's confidence …

"Well, I really must be running on," said Roach. "I was looking for someplace else. But I can always come back some other day."

"Wh-what were you looking for? May-maybe I can help you."

"Nothing important. An address on Split Tree Circle."

"My, my house is on Split Tree Circle. I can, can, can show you where it is! See, it's off Split Tree Lane, so a lot of people get lo-lost. I-I-I will be glad to show you where it is, Mr., um …"

"LaRoche." The demon extended his hand. "Johnny LaRoche."

Heeere's Johnny!

"M-my name is Ferguson. Floyd Ferguson. Ve-very pleased to meet you, Mr. LaRoche."

"The pleasure is mine. May I call you Floyd?"

"Su-sure, Johnny! Lots of people get mixed up. Because th-there is no more split tree there. There, there was once. When I was lit-tle. But it got a tr-tree disease and had-had to be cut down. There-there is my house, right there, num-ber sev-en."

Roach was looking at number 2. *The Kavanaugh house.* There were items of men's clothing and shattered golf clubs strewn over the front lawn.

"Floyd, would you know what the story is behind that?"

"They, they, they had a terrible fight. Last night. The Kav-kavanaughs. Now, Mo-mother said if I ca-can't say something nice about so-someone else, do-don't say no-nothing at all. But … come on in my house. I, I will tell you what hap-pened."

It was no surprise to Roach that Ferguson's house was the one with sagging gutters, patches of dead grass, and peeling paint. "Co-come on in. Would you like some soda pop? So-some po-tato chips, Johnny?"

"If it's no trouble."

"No-no trouble at all." Ferguson got the refreshments out of the kitchen.

"Mo-mother al-ways told me I was too, too trust-ing. That-that I had to be care-ful about who I let-let in here. But, but you look like su-such a nice person, Johnny."

"I'm glad you think so, Floyd. Now what can you tell me about the Kavanaughs?"

"Well, Mr. Kavanaugh is an at-torney, and he's mar-ried to Mrs. Kavanaugh, only she's kind of mean. Wo-won't talk to me. And they have two kids in special school. But-but not like the special school I went to. These kids are in a special smart school."

All of this was news to Roach. "What about last night?" he asked.

"Oh, Mr. Kavanaugh ca-came home from work late. And, and, him and his wife started yelling at each other. So loud I could hear. Then-then the front door opened, and she pushed him out. She called him crazy. Crazier than I am. Johnny, may-maybe I, I, I am a lit-tle odd. But I'm not really crazy. I do-don't know why she said that."

"Did you hear anything else?"

"No, just lots of screaming and yelling. And then Mrs. Kavanaugh opened the upstairs win-window and threw all his stuff out. And said she was gonna get a div-orce. So he, he gave up. Picked up so-some of his stuff and drove away. I don't know where he went."

"Kavanaugh's in a lot of trouble," Roach observed and thought, *Good. Jerk had it coming, after the trouble he caused me.*

"I'll show you some-thing," Ferguson continued. "See their driveway? That's her van. But the other car? The Acura? Not his. It belongs to her sis-ter. Grace. She's a nurse. I think she's gonna stay there. A while."

"Interesting," said Roach.

"Want more potato chips?"

"That'd be nice."

Floyd refilled the bowl. "Johnny?"

"Yes?"

"Do you mind if, if I ask you some-thing per-sonal?"

Am I what I appear to be? I'm not going to answer that one.

"Depends on the question."

"Well, um ... are you ma-married?"

"No. Never had time for that sort of thing. In my job, I travel a lot."

"Ever ... ever have a girl?"

"Same thing. I'm not the type who settles down."

"Oh. That's sad. I've never been married either. Or had a girl. But, but, but, there was this one time ..."

Roach thought, *Spare me this idiocy!*

"There was this girl. Her name was Michelle. I lo-loved, her Johnny. But, but then I found out she was married. To a nor-normal guy. Not like me. She was ha-happy with him. So, I guess it's okay. But I wish, lots of times, I wish she'd ma-married me instead. We could li-live in this nice big house. We could have a fa-family. Maybe not smart like the Kavanaugh kids. But I'd love them, Johnny. And I'd take care of them. I gu-guess it wasn't meant to be. But it's ha-hard, Johnny. Hard, being alone. Don't you think?"

Floyd Ferguson had served his final purpose. Roach had to give up. His plan was ruined. He could put Ferguson out of his misery. But there was no way he could sink his talons into such an incorrupt soul.

He swallowed one more potato chip and went to the door.

"Johnny?" Floyd asked.

Roach changed into a visible manifestation of his real form. "Oh my dear Lord!" Ferguson screamed as his aorta exploded. Blood burst out of his orifices, spattering all over the living room. Roach managed to dodge it. He waited till the empty shell of a body lay still.

He then went through the house, making sure all the windows were shut tight. Then he turned the furnace back on and cranked the heat up to ninety. He shut the front door firmly and made sure it was locked.

In a few days, the neighbors would notice the odor. Sooner or later, someone would call the cops. Maybe that Kavanaugh dame. Serve her right.

Which reminded him to hurry back to his den and analyze the latest data about Kathleen Kavanaugh. What he had seen already told him that Kathleen was nervous, submissive, ruled by fears. The shambles in her yard told a different story. She just might be a handful.

In the meantime, he did have a girl, and her name was Dorothy. They were going to have lots more fun. And besides, he'd done his bad deed for the day. What more do you expect from him?

12

Kathleen was curled up on the couch, sobbing, but listening to her sister's words.

"I know what you want to say, Grace! *I told you so!*"

"I'd never say that, sis. Now all along, I've had my misgivings about Larry. But I'm never going to say that, no. He was, after all, your lawfully wedded husband. Even if he told lots of lies. Lies that people want to hear. Still, lies."

"Soon to be my ex!" Kathleen gulped.

"But I'm your sister! And I've known you a hell of a lot longer than he has, right?"

Kathleen nodded, yes.

"And maybe I understand you a little better?"

Another nod, yes.

"What you did tonight was the right thing. He pushed you over the limit. And you threw that clown out. You told him the truth about himself. Larry Kavanaugh is a liar, a con man, a fraud, and it's time someone told him. Because you know why?"

Kathleen shook her head, no.

"Because, as Mother used to say, you and I are cut from the same bolt of cloth. We're just a pair of Irish bitches. And tonight, you got in touch with your inner Irish bitch. And it was beautiful."

Kathleen sat up. "You never did like him, did you?"

"Mother and I were never members of the Larry Kavanaugh fan club. Of which there appears to be only one member."

"You know," Kathleen said, pointing to the shards of their mother's favorite vase, "he did that."

"Yes, and I know that next time it's going to be you or the kids, or all three at once. Only, there's never going to be a next time. Am I right?"

"As always. What about the kids?"

"I got them into their jammies. They're finally sleeping. You know, they are extraordinary. And they did not get their smarts from their dad."

"You think of everything."

"In my job? I'd better! Got any tea?"

"Of course! Spoken like a true Irish bitch."

"That's the spirit!"

The McGrath sisters retreated to the kitchen table. "Now let me get this straight," Grace said as Kathleen served tea. "What exactly did El Cheapo tell you he did that was so awful?"

"Sold his soul to the devil, then expected me to believe him."

"Wow! I think that if there were any evil spirits involved, they must have been on his breath. Were they?"

"Actually, I didn't smell any alcohol."

"He said that when he was stone-cold sober? You're right; that takes the cake."

Kathleen stirred her tea. "You're still Catholic, aren't you?"

"Yep, in spite of everything, I still am a good Catholic girl. Can't deny it. I go to that new place, St. Teresa of Kolkata. You still on the outs?"

"That sums me up. And Larry. But you know, he has a phobia of collection plates."

"He'd better develop a phobia of divorce court."

"But, Grace, in your experience, does this sort of thing ever happen? I mean, right now, not in the Dark Ages?"

"We had a patient in the ER recently who claimed to be possessed by seven demons," she admitted. "Turns out, high on drugs. No, in my experience, and I've seen a lot, we don't look for any supernatural cause, without going down the list of natural causes. This is nothing but my speculation, based on what I know so far. Larry is lying. Again. Or he had some sort of dealings with a scam artist. Lost his shirt and is trying to keep you from finding out. I mean, the whole thing is so far-fetched. And with his track record?"

"I am an attorney! I'm going to star in a major motion picture! Miracle Furniture!"

"I just would not trust him as far as I could throw him. I've known this for quite some time, sis. And now you know it too. See, prayer works!"

"I guess it does. There are times, Grace, I've envied you for your faith. But still."

"But still what?"

"I guess I'm not as trusting as you are of any higher power."

"Then it's a good thing you're not an alcoholic."

"I suppose so! I think … at first, I fell for Larry's stories. About himself. About the celebrities he says he knew and didn't. So, I fell in love with him. Or thought I was in love. But maybe I was trying all along to make him my higher power. My protector. All along, I've been so afraid. And I thought having Larry around made me safe."

Grace poured a bit more tea. "Of what, sis?"

"I have this thing about, well, people who are not mentally right. Like Flakey, down the way."

"You mean the guy in that ratty-looking house?"

"He's the one."

"Okay. Now how long have you lived here?"

"About ten years."

"And how long has this Flakey lived over there?"

"I think he's always lived there. At first with his mother, but she's not there anymore."

"And in all this time, Flakey didn't strike out at anyone?"

"Well, no. He's probably harmless, but I was scared of him anyway, and I thought having Larry around made me feel safe, just in case he did."

"So, you solved the Flakey problem by making a worse one. You get where I'm coming from?"

"Stop making sense!"

"Look, sis, I know you don't like to talk about this. So, I haven't said anything. Yet. Watch out. I'm about to. Did Flakey remind you of Jimmy? Is that who you're really afraid of?"

Kathleen dabbed at her eyes. "Yes. I've always been terrified of

Jimmy. I kept thinking that one day he'd get loose and come over here. Then what would I do without Larry to protect me?"

Grace nodded. "Okay. I didn't want to tell you this before. I didn't want to upset you. But Jimmy's been dead for three years."

"Good Lord!"

"He died on Christmas day. I understood why you never wanted to see him again. But I did see him. Occasionally. The care he was getting in that dump was abysmal. I complained about it, for all the good that did. And his condition gradually got worse and worse. He developed massive decubitus ulcers. That's Medicalese for bedsores. And after a while, infection set in, he died, and that was that."

"Oh, Grace! All this time, and I had no idea!"

"I know your perception of Jimmy was different from mine. All you saw was an irrational destructive force on the loose."

"King Kong in New York. Godzilla in Tokyo. The kids love those films, but they creep me out. Jimmy is why."

"Maybe because you were closer to him in age. I was so much younger. So, I saw him in a different light."

"How so?"

"I don't recall seeing him as dangerous or violent. I thought it was odd that he was so big but acted like a little kid. And that's how Jimmy and I related to each other. Two little kids. We had some good times together before everything fell apart."

"I should have realized, when the two of you built your tree house."

"I designed it, but Jimmy did all the hard work. I was too young to understand why other children were not allowed to come to our house and play with us. I would have been terribly lonesome without Jimmy. I was confused, scared, when they took him away."

"All I felt was relief."

"Yeah, but ..." Grace poured a bit more tea. "Once I grew up enough to understand, I went through old records, trying to make sense of what really went down. Do you recall the name Isaiah Jones?"

"Um, no."

"He was the young fellow Jimmy killed. He'd just graduated from high school. Had a college scholarship. Was going to go into premed. He just happened to be hanging around with his pals at the bus stop when

Jimmy got off the bus. Another example of a nice African American kid in the wrong place at the wrong time."

"And I never even thought about him!"

"Yeah, well, I have. He's on my prayer list, if you want to know the truth. So is his mother. I can't even imagine her loss."

"Neither can I," said Kathleen, thinking of Bobby.

"I read a lot of the old articles and transcripts. Oh, it was bad, Kathleen. I mean, we were both traumatized, but what Mom and Dad went through was so much worse. The scandal, the shame."

"We weren't allowed to watch the news on TV."

"But you know the worst part? That Walsh creature."

"I never forgot about her."

"The only good thing was it was like our fifteen minutes of fame. Once that was over, something rotten had to happen to somebody else. Attention's fickle. It got diverted to the next thing."

"Not for Dorothy!"

"Yeah, she actually used to come to the kindergarten class to harass me. The nuns used to chase her away. But do you remember the part about the big recital coming up?"

"It got cancelled, didn't it? Lots of the other kids were disappointed. They had parts in it. Dancing Hershey's kisses."

"Dorothy's fault. She was going to be the star."

"What was she supposed to sing? 'Animal Crackers in My Soup'?"

Grace laughed. "No, another Shirley Temple classic. 'On the Good Ship Lollipop.'"

"Oh, gross!"

"That was the sweet Dorothy for you. She was going to be the star. Superstar, but she didn't get far! Because Mother Superior knew the way she was treating the two of us. And threw her out of school on her tight little ass. So, no recital. Too damn bad."

Kathleen had to laugh. "I just knew she was gone, and I was so glad of it! But I'll tell you something, Grace. I was always afraid of her."

"Afraid of that waste of human DNA? What for?"

"Because she knows what went down. And I've seen her a few times since I married Larry. And the last time, oh, it was a while ago, but she threatened me."

"She did what!"

"She saw the kids. And asked me if they knew about Jimmy. Grace, I've always kept it a secret from them. Wasn't it bad enough, what we went through? I want to spare them all that. But Dorothy asked me if I had told them. Said it would be a shame if they found out by accident."

"That's blackmail! Did she ever get any money out of you?"

"No, and I have not seen her since. It's been at least five years. However, I do keep up with her."

"How?"

"I read this newsletter from St. Catherine's. She very active there."

"Let me see that! Oh my God, look at that face! That grin will never change. You know something, Kathleen? There ought to be a copy of this picture in every post office! Let's see what she's up to!"

Grace read, then threw the letter on the kitchen table. "Sis, I'm sorry, but this is a scream! Look at Dorothy! She has this great love for the babies, doesn't she? Until they get born. After that, you're on your own, kid. Tough luck!"

"I guess I never thought of it that way."

"I did. And that's why I personally don't go in for this sort of thing. Does more harm than good, if you ask me. And Dorothy's still damn good at doing harm. Can you imagine being stuck on an airplane with her all the way to DC?"

"You would earn a martyr's crown."

"Listen, she tries to pull anything, you tell me. We go straight to the cops, you hear me?"

Kathleen nodded.

"Now, look. It's way past midnight. And you've had a tough day and another one tomorrow. Above all, you need a lawyer. I can help you get one."

"Grace, I know your church does not approve of divorce."

"Holy Mother Church is getting a bit more understanding. Even if it does take another thousand years. It's getting a bit clearer that you don't have to get dragged through Hell to get to Heaven. And you are not supposed to drag your kids through Hell with you."

Kathleen nodded.

"Now, it just so happens I know a divorce lawyer. He's helped a lot of my friends at the hospital."

"Is he good? Suppose Larry tries to get custody of the kids?"

"He's so good his screen name is PitBull222."

"I like him already."

"If you don't mind, I'll spend the rest of the night here."

"I wish you could stay for a while, for the sake of the kids. At least till the dust settles."

"I could do that, sis. Just one thing. I don't want to have to board the cats at the vet. So, if you and the kids don't mind, can they come here with me?"

"Are you kidding? You know how much Bobby and Jeanine love Dante and Virgil!"

13

Dorothy Walsh was flustered. That dream she had, it felt so real! Someone was speaking clearly to her. Even though she could not recall his all of his exact words, his spirit was both ancient and wise. And he cared so deeply about her. He wanted her to have all the things she was so unfairly denied. He had to be her guardian angel.

He told her amazing things. Kathleen Kavanaugh was afraid of her. She, therefore, had a lot more power over Kathleen than she had realized. It was time to act on it.

Dorothy sat down at her desk and got out a box of her personal stationery. She did not know Kathleen's address, but that was easily found online.

Kavanaugh, Lawrence & Kathleen, 2 Split Tree Circle

She addressed an envelope, then got out a fresh sheet of paper, endowed with her favorite scent, April in Paris.

Dear Kathleen,

I feel it is wrong that we have been estranged for so many years. I would like to see more of you and your darling children. Your daughter is the spitting image of you! Perhaps we could have lunch together soon; my treat, of course.

I do wish to have a discussion on a topic of mutual interest. As you know, I am concerned about your children's well-being. I cannot help but recall all of that unpleasantness that occurred when we were both in second grade. I feel that it is in the best interest of both children that they be told all of the facts as soon as possible. Were they to find out at a future time, it could be quite upsetting.

If you feel you cannot disclose this matter to them yourself, I would most certainly be willing to explain to them, as gently as possible, what the charges against Jimmy entailed and what he did to the unfortunate Isaiah.

Furthermore, it is my belief that if you refuse to tell them, you are not acting in their best interest. If you then refuse to allow me to speak with them, I will understand, but I will require an initial payment of $20,000, cash, in small bills. Kindly place them in a plain brown bag and leave it in the hollow tree by the swing set in the park.

This and all subsequent payments will go into an escrow account for their future psychotherapy. I care about you, Kathleen, but you are failing as a mother if you do not deal honestly with those children. And I will not stand by and let this occur!

Yours most sincerely,
Dorothy Marie Walsh

Direct and to the point. Dorothy folded it, placed it into the envelope, and sealed it. Suddenly she felt as if a light went off in her brain. In the back of her head, she felt the presence of her guardian angel.

"Dorothy! No!"

Suppose, just suppose, that Kathleen were not really afraid of her? That she took the letter to the police? They'd have Dorothy's name, address, phone number, email address, Twitter handle, handwriting sample, even her signature scent! They'd be pounding down the door so fast!

"Don't mail it till you hear back from me! I have a little more research to do. No, don't rip it up; just keep it in a safe spot for now."

Trembling, Dorothy stuffed the letter into her desk drawer.

After all, she had seen something on TV once called *Stupid Crooks*. How humiliating to be included with them. Her guardian angel would not let that happen.

Dorothy tried to recall more of the dream. Yes, there was more, wasn't there? Something about Larry Kavanaugh. Her face turned a brilliant red.

Larry Kavanaugh had been making love to her, in her own little beddy-bye.

Oh my!

She had never thought that much about Larry. Certainly never felt attracted to him.

Not until now.

She tried to bring up memories of him. At least the way he looked in college. In fact, he was kind of cute, with that dimple in his chin.

He was certainly charming. And if everything he said did not always check out, what did it matter? In fact, the stories he told were rather appealing in their way. Kathleen fell in love with him, didn't she?

Oh, I must not think of such things! He is, after all, married and father of at least two. And my virginity means the world to me!

What to do? This required a lot of thought. At least she had that strange sense of connection with her guardian angel. She could ask him for his guidance. Then, she went back to thinking about Larry Kavanaugh's fingers, reaching behind her, unhooking her bra.

14

Upon leaving Split Tree Circle, Larry had spent the rest of the night in a motel on Route 3. What a hovel. The walls looked moldy. The stained sheets reeked of other people's tobacco.

When he got up in the morning, the first thing he saw was a huge and heavily armored cockroach in the tub. Running around like he owned the joint. He probably did. Larry made a note not to spend another night in this dump. Yet the cockroach refreshed his memory.

"Johnny LaRoche! That was the demon's name. Not Stink Bug."

Larry then moved on to a succession of motels, waiting for Kathleen to call and apologize so they could reconcile. Her call never came.

Yet he still had his needs, even if Kathleen was neglecting her wifely duty. He had already cheated on her several times. No big deal, just one-night stands. One evening, he sat in the Round Robin Bar, near his office, hoping for some action. A pretty girl caught his eye, and he winked at her. She approached him.

"Well, hello there!" he said.

"Lawrence P. Kavanaugh?"

"That's me! Can I buy you a drink?"

Instead, she handed him an envelope. He willingly took it.

"Have a nice day," she said and turned and left. Only then did he realize she was a process server. Attorney Pit Bull took his first bite.

After that, he moved into an apartment with a month-to-month lease. Only once did he return to Split Tree Circle, to pick up the rest of his things on the front lawn, plus his own important papers and a locked metal box from his rolltop desk. He groaned when he saw the Acura in his driveway.

"Goofy Grace! Oh no!"

Kathleen opened the door without comment. Those cats were running around the living room. Grace was yakking on the phone.

"Bobby and Jeanine home from school yet?" he muttered.

"They'll be back any minute."

"Can I at least say hello to my own kids?"

"No funny stuff," Kathleen warned him.

"I know," he snarled. "Pit Bull is watching me. And he ain't no Santa Claus."

Grace ended her call. "That was Mr. Stink Bug," she said. "He lost his pitchfork and thinks he left it here."

"You are a riot!"

At that moment, he saw his children coming up the front steps. "Hey, Mom?" Bobby called.

"Yes, dear?"

"Something stinks!"

"All right, Kathleen, I've had it! I have not seen my children in how long? And this is how they talk to me? They tell me I stink? This is what you told them to say? I think that as their father, I'm due a bit more respect!"

Larry tossed his things into his car and took off as his astonished children watched.

"Sheeesh, fine damn way to act," Grace said.

"Well, gee, Mom! Gee, Aunt Grace! All I said was something stinks. I didn't mean Dad!"

"Yes, well, you know how he takes everything so personally."

"Mom," said Jeanine, "Bobby's telling the truth. We took a short cut when we got off the bus. We went by Mr. Ferguson's house. And there's a bad smell over there like you would not believe!"

"I mean, it totally reeks," Bobby added.

"It's probably nothing," said Kathleen. "You know, he's not the best housekeeper in the world. Probably some wild animal got into his crawl space and died, that's all. The bad smell will go away."

"I'll go do a quick check on it," Grace offered. "Bobby and Jeanine can play red dot with Dante and Virgil."

Dante was the noble Florentine in his brown striped coat. Virgil, solid white, looked like he'd just come through Inferno in an immaculate toga.

Grace returned after a while. The children and the cats were still whooping it up in the family room. Grace called her sister aside.

"Well? Could you smell what they were talking about?"

"Whew! Did I ever! Kathleen, you may be right, that it might be a dead raccoon or possum in the crawl space. But, um, when did you last see him, what did you call him?"

"Flakey Ferguson?"

"Yeah, Flakey."

"Oh, I don't know! Over a week, maybe two. Why?"

Grace lowered her voice to a whisper. "I'm worried."

"But why?"

"I talked to some of your other neighbors, and they haven't seen him at all. They were getting upset about the odor too. And I thought it was a little weird, now that the weather's getting better, all his windows and doors were shut tight."

"Flakey's more than a little weird."

"Nobody's checked up on him?"

"I wouldn't know."

"Does he have a phone?"

"I wouldn't know that either."

Grace got on the computer and looked his number up. "All I find is an Irene Ferguson at that address."

"Must be his mother. She's gone."

"Hmmm. I'm going to give our friend Flakey a buzz."

"But why?"

"C'mere. I don't want the kids to hear this, but I've smelled that smell before."

"Grace, surely you don't think!"

Grace dialed the number.

"Suppose he answers?" Kathleen asked.

"At least we'll know he's alive. I'll say I'm selling something."

"Suppose he wants to buy it?"

Grace hung up. "Voice mail," she said. "A woman's voice, must be Mama. It's time for a welfare check. That means I get the cops to see what's going on in there. No emergency, no 911, I just ask them to make sure everything's kosher dill."

Grace called the police nonemergency number. "He's a single male, lives alone, known eccentric, has not been seen in a while. There is a foul odor present. Seven Split Tree Circle. I'm the sister of one of the neighbors. I'm a registered nurse. I'll meet you by his front yard."

"Oh, Grace, I certainly hope it's nothing!"

"So do I, sis. So do I."

A prowl car arrived in fifteen minutes. There were two cops. Frank was fat. Charley was skinny. "Here it is, number seven," she told them.

"And what's his name?"

"Ferguson."

They went up on the porch, rang the doorbell, pounded on the door, and shouted, "Mr. Ferguson?" No response. "Charley," Frank said, "Can you see in the window at all?"

Charley got out a rag, wiped the dirty window, and squinted into the living room.

"Mother of God! He's on the floor, and there's blood spatters up to the ceiling. Call for backup."

Grace got out her cell and called her sister. "Keep the kids inside. No matter what they hear, and it's going to get loud. They don't need to see this."

15

Dorothy had waited to hear from her guardian angel, and sure enough, she heard him in the back of her head.

"You still have that letter to Kathleen?"

"In my desk drawer. Do you need me to mail it now?"

"No! Keep it where it is until I tell you to! Listen carefully, Dorothy. I need you to be somewhere else at about four this afternoon. Do you know where the Round Robin Bar is?"

"Why, yes, but ... a barroom?"

"Yes, a barroom! I need you to go there alone!"

"Oh my!" Dorothy had a low opinion of women who walked, unescorted, into bars. That was no way to retain one's eternal virginity.

"Trust me on this one, Dorothy. There will be a surprise there, just for you. You need this, Dorothy. And go dressed up nicely. In the meantime, I'll find something even better, just for you, if you go to the Round Robin like I say."

"Well, all right."

Roach broke the connection. And boy, was she going to get a fun surprise. Yet Roach had even bigger plans for his protégé.

At least Dorothy understood she could end up on a program like *Stupid Crooks*. That was not going to happen. From what Roach had learned of Kathleen, she had changed from a pathetic mouse into a roaring lioness. Try blackmailing her, and she'd rip your head off.

There were other things, though, such as Dorothy's case of the hots for Larry Kavanaugh. Scorch wasn't kidding about that elixir.

Still, there was more. Last night, Roach had again been watching his flat-screen TV. And what was this? A program called *Sing! Sing! Sing!*

It appeared to be some sort of elimination contest. The grand prize was a recording contract. Fame and stardom! The ultimate revenge on all who had wronged her! How special would that be? And didn't Dorothy deserve as much?

Dorothy went through her closet. Her best dresses were for wearing to Mass at St. Catherine's. They were far too modest for a place like the Round Robin. She ran off to the mall and bought something more risqué, a pair of open-toe high heels, then a push-up bra and matching thong at Victoria's Secret. She had her nails done and hair restyled at the salon. This day cost her plenty. Yet it ought to please her guardian angel.

When she got home, it was almost time to leave. She took a shower, liberally applied April in Paris, and changed into her new outfit.

"Oh my!" The low neckline, plus her new bra, showed off assets she never knew she had. As a last step, she removed her religious medal and replaced it with a gold chain. As she drove to the Round Robin, "Love Potion Number Nine" was playing on the radio.

Already the Round Robin was crowded, for happy hour had commenced. A man behind her said, "Woo! Woo!" But where was the surprise her guardian angel had promised?

There! Larry Kavanaugh, and he was all alone at the bar, nursing a scotch and water. Dorothy sauntered up to him.

"Well, hi there! Don't think I've seen you in here before. Have a seat. Can I get you something?"

"That's very kind of you. If it's not too much trouble, I'll have a grasshopper."

"Grasshopper it is, for the little lady."

"But you have seen me before."

"Yeah? Where?"

"It's been a while, but remember Joe's Grill? When you were at St. Augustine, and I was at Our Lady of Grace?"

Larry twitched at bit at the word grace but gazed into his drink as if searching for the answer. "Let me see now … Joe's Grill … wait a sec … can't be … Dorothy Walsh?"

"The very one."

"Can't believe it! Didn't you become a nun?"

"Well, yes, I was, for a while …"

There was another resentment. Dorothy had been a postulant in the Sisters of Divine Compassion. She did not last long enough to take her temporary vows. There was an issue of her being unsuited for community life, totally unfounded. The novice mistress had been out to get her.

"Well, you sure don't look like no nun now. You look terrific! How ya been?"

"I'm doing quite well, in fact."

"You still sing? I remember that about you."

"In fact, I do. And you, Larry? You were in prelaw."

"Yes, I'm an attorney now."

"I heard you got married."

"Yeah, well ..."

Dorothy's grasshopper was served, and she took a big gulp.

"Yep. I married Kathleen McGrath, sad to say."

"Sad?"

"We lasted a while. But it's over now. She, um, she just threw me out of the house. And now she's gone and filed for a divorce."

"Oh, Larry, I am so sorry to hear that!" The alcohol going down made the lie easier to come up. Dorothy took another gulp of green liquid.

"I did everything for her, got her everything she could possibly want, a nice house on Split Tree Circle. Not good enough. She wanted an estate in Swan Pointe, can you believe? With a pool in the backyard."

Dorothy edged closer. "Any children?"

"Two. One of each. She's got them in this private science school. Sure costs me a lot. I did everything for her and those kids. I guess this is the thanks I get. Damn shame. I tried to make a go of the marriage, but ..."

Dorothy drained the grasshopper. "Want another?" Larry offered.

"Actually, I'd rather talk to you, Larry. Someplace quieter."

Then he offered, "My place or yours, Dorothy? What do you say?"

Dorothy did not want her place. Too many pictures of St. Theresa of the Roses.

"Your place will be fine."

"Not much, just a lousy efficiency apartment."

"I don't mind." The upper part of her was saying, *No, no, no.* The lower part was fully engulfed in flames for Larry Kavanaugh.

Larry paid up his tab. "I'll get us a taxi."

"Never mind. My car's out front."

"Let's go."

The radio station was now playing Frank Sinatra, singing of strangers in the night. Larry's place, such as it was, was not far from the Round Robin. His apartment was right on the first floor. The minute they got inside, he had his tongue down her throat.

"Oh my. Oh, Larry." No one had ever done that to her before. It destroyed her reason. He reached behind her and pulled down her zipper. She wiggled out of the rest of her outfit as Larry tossed his clothes around. Then he opened up the sofa bed and lowered her onto it.

"It's been … so long … my wife … such a cold fish."

Nothing seemed real, except these sweet sensations. What Dorothy could not see was that Roach was drifting over Larry's bare butt with a video camera. He was doing a live feed to Scorch, who had it on a screen in Hell. Every seat in the Judas Iscariot aula was filled with demons shrieking catcalls and suggestions.

"Go for it, Larry! Do! Be! Do! Be! Do!"

Larry heard nothing but Dorothy's sighs of delight, mixing with the squeaks of the sofa bed.

"What do you want of me, darling?" he moaned.

"All, I beg you, please!"

Her sighs turned into sweet musical notes. When Larry rammed through her virginity, Dorothy let loose a perfect C, over high C.

And all of Hades rose up and gave her a standing ovation.

16

Blood. They both dreamed of it. So much blood. Spattered up to the ceiling.

Larry woke up at dawn and wondered for a moment who this strange woman in his sofa bed was. He turned on the lamp and pulled down the sheet.

He remembered her name. Dorothy Something-or-Other. He had known her in college so long ago. She had been such a Goody Two-shoes, was going to be a nun. Then he saw the bottom sheet was stained with a puddle of blood.

"Oh wow. Dorothy?" He woke her up.

"Yes, darling?"

"I, um, I didn't know that you were a virgin. I would have been more careful."

"You don't have to be such a gentleman." Gazing on him drowned out the small voice in her head that said, *He's still legally married. Children are involved. This is not a sacred union; it's a mortal sin, what you did.* Dorothy replied to that voice with the words of Debbie Boone from "You Light Up My Life": *"It can't be wrong, when it feels so right."*

"Well, um, it's past six. And I do have to get to work today, much as I'd like to stay with you."

What a hot little number she was! The best yet!

"I guess you do." She had no clothes besides the items still tossed on the floor, so covered herself in Larry's pajama top. "I'll make us breakfast. What have we got?"

Larry showed her the galley kitchen, then turned the TV on to the local news channel.

"A spokesman for the congressman had no further comment," the anchorman said. "In other news, police uncovered a horrifying scene when they were called for a routine check in a quiet suburban neighborhood. News 8's Meg Linton has more. Meg?"

"Yes, Bob, we're here on Split Tree Circle, where police were summoned to check on the well-being of Floyd Ferguson, the resident of this house."

Larry sprang up. "Did she say Split Tree Circle?"

Behind the reporter, the Ferguson house was sealed off in yellow crime scene tape. There was a plywood cover nailed to the front door. Meg interviewed one of the police. "The victim is a single disabled man, lived alone. He was quiet and kept to himself. No one can recall for sure when he was last seen. It may take a while to determine the cause of death, as the remains were in an advanced state of decomposition. There was evidence of massive blood loss, so we will be treating this as a homicide. We ask that if you have any information, to call us on the tip line at the bottom of your screen."

The reporter turned to the camera. "Neighbors tell me that Mr. Ferguson was known to be a bit eccentric but peaceful. He would not hurt a fly. No enemies. No one can make any sense of this. Again, if you have any information, you can leave an anonymous tip. Back to you, Bob."

"Split Tree Circle is where I live," Larry muttered, "or used to live."

"Did you know this Floyd Ferguson?"

"No. Not really. I don't think anyone did. A loner. Kathleen called him Flakey. Weird, but like they said, never hurt anything or anyone."

Dorothy whispered, "Do you think he was actually murdered?"

"I don't know, honey. I'd better get to the office. Right away. And you better get dressed."

"Oh dear, oh dear," Dorothy lamented.

"And by the way," Larry said, "write down your phone number. I never did get it."

17

It was as if all of Split Tree Circle had died.

There was no longer a sound of children playing, no one taking a dog for a walk. Only dead silence. A prowl car remained by the Ferguson house. No one lingered on the sidewalk. The crime scene tape had been taken down at number 7. A cleanup crew, specializing in violent crime, had finished. At least the odor was gone.

Grace went back to her sister's house after the police were done talking with her. There were news crews present, but Grace was not about to put her face on camera in the matter of a potential violent crime.

By then, the kids were in bed. "Bobby's sleeping with Dante, and Jeanine's got Virgil," Kathleen told her. "I'm so glad to have those cats! So, what did you see?"

"What little I did see, oh boy, pretty bad. I know, I'm a nurse, I'm supposed to be shock-proof. But nobody really is. A lot of blood. Wide spatter pattern. Like he tied to fight off somebody stabbing him. That's what the cops are going on now."

"At least they didn't say that on TV."

"Yeah, well, I think the kids have heard about enough." Kathleen sighed. "You know, I feel so bad about this. As if it's in some way my fault!"

"Come on, sis. If you didn't stab him, how are you at fault?"

"I was the one who gave him that nickname, Flakey. I was always mocking him, making jokes about all those quirks he couldn't help. Funny jokes. I made people laugh at him. So, I think that I isolated him from everyone else. And if something was bothering him, there was no one he could reach out to for help. And I'm so sorry. Grace. He's dead now, and I'm so terribly sorry about the way I treated him." Kathleen wiped her nose. "You're lucky; if you were in my shoes, you could get absolution."

"Yeah, well," said Grace.

"I mean, I ask myself, who would hurt Flakey? I'm sorry, Floyd. What's the point of such evil? Did the cops tell you anything?"

"They can't tell me anything more. But I know the motive could not have been robbery. There was nothing in that house worth more than a dime."

"I don't know. You read about some people who live like that. Then it turns out they have a million dollars in the mattress."

"I don't think Floyd will turn out to be one of them. There's something else, though, that they're not going to put on the news, so keep quiet about this, will you?"

"Of course."

"His thermostat was turned up to ninety. That made the whole process of decomposition go a lot faster."

"Very odd," said Kathleen.

"Now, we don't know. Was it always that hot in there? Maybe Floyd liked it hot. Or maybe someone deliberately did it to destroy as much evidence as possible."

"If he was on a fixed income, I doubt he'd be able to afford a sky-high energy bill."

"Which points to someone else's doing it. But all of this is speculation. Second-guessing. Floyd's with the medical examiner now. That's where he needs to be. Dr. Whitney's doing the autopsy, and he really knows his stuff. Remember when they excavated for the mall and dug up a slave burial ground? Dr. Whitney took over and figured out why a lot of them died. After more than a hundred years. So, let's not get all worried, for the sake of the kids."

"We'll know soon enough."

"Right. Hear anything from Larry? He must have seen it on TV."

"Nope. Nothing. As to what he's doing now, Rhett Butler said it best. Frankly, I don't give a damn."

"Hold that thought," Grace advised her.

18

Two dudes in casual clothing entered the mall and headed for Best Buy. One was Johnny LaRoche. His friend, a techie from Kolkata, was calling himself Kumar. Kumar wore a turban and a T-shirt that said Computer Repair. The purchased a top-of-the-line DVD player and some blank discs and paid for them with Johnny's perfectly good credit card. (Which meant that their purchases would never be paid for at all.)

Johnny drove them back to his place. They stopped off and bought some beer and pretzels with the same card. Then, back in Johnny's apartment, they could drop all pretense and be themselves: Roach and Scorch, demons.

Scorch unboxed the DVD player and hooked it up to Roach's flat-screen TV, then inserted one of his own discs. "This is going to blow your mind," he promised, and hit Play.

"It's been … so long … my wife … such a cold fish."

"That's the guy who sold himself to you?" Scorch asked.

"That's the one."

"Look at the bare ass on him."

"I can see his hemorrhoids up there!"

"I'm telling you, Roach, this equipment is state of the art, all the way. Every detail, just right."

"He was a bargain, and that boss of ours, still not satisfied."

"Wait! Here comes the good part."

"What do you want of me, darling?"

"All, I beg you, please!"

"You got it, toots!" Roach told the image of Dorothy.

Scorch had to lower the volume to keep the neighbors from hearing that high note. "Now! He's in like Errol Flynn."

"Go for it!" They set up a chant of woo, woo, woo! Scorch laughed so hard he spat out a mixture of beer and pretzel.

"Ka-boom!" said Roach.

"Darling, you are the very best," Dorothy moaned.

"Yeah, but what's she got to compare him with?" Scorch asked.

"Good point," said Roach.

The recording came to an end. "Good bye, consecrated virgin. Hello, porn star," Scorch noted.

"Don't you have to rewind that?" Roach asked.

"Nope. Those days are long gone." Scorch ejected the DVD.

"So how are things in Hell?" Roach asked. "They miss me yet?"

"Satan sure does. He's still out to get you."

"Tough. I got him Larry Kavanaugh dirt cheap, and he didn't appreciate it."

"You know what his problem is? He never thinks outside the box. He's like a crabby old man in that office of his. Only comes out to say, 'You kids! Get off my lawn!' Whereas, you? You showed him some original thought, striking out on your own. And once you best him at his own game, you know how he gets."

"Jealous."

"And how! Then he starts obsessing."

"He must think I'm doing better than I really am."

"Looks to me like you're doing all right."

"Yeah, well, that last one could have been better."

"How do you mean?"

"I got outsmarted by the medical examiner. I could not get the soul. So, I destroyed the body and turned the heat all the way up. So, he'd rot fast, you follow me?"

"Makes sense."

"All of those neighbors who wouldn't even give him the time of day thought he'd been murdered in his own house. That's what it looked like. Scared them good! It should have worked. But that medical examiner still found that he died of an aortic aneurism and signed off on a natural death."

"Oh well," Scorch said, "win a few, lose a few."

"And the rest got rained out."

"How's it going with that connector?"

"Oh, yeah, I wanted to ask you about that. At first, it was great. Gave me a good strong connection to our little porn star and got the virus into her archenemy, Kathleen, who turns out to be married to lover boy."

"A married man, carrying on like that!" said Scorch. "I feel faint! Quick, my smelling salts!"

"The virus worked fine in Kathleen. For a while. Gave me a good baseline of her personality. Timid little wifey, scared of her own shadow. Then when she blew up at him and threw him out, all of a sudden, I couldn't get a signal. Just a snapping sound and then nothing. And nothing but static since."

"Hunh!" said Scorch. "Remind me to have a look at that when I get back to the lab. What was the hate connection between wifey and porn star? Did you find that out?"

"Goes way back. Seems there was some scandal in Kathleen's family when she was about seven. Lots of ugly publicity."

"The best kind," said Scorch.

"Those two were in the same school, and Dorothy was the class mean girl even then. Well, Dorothy got kicked out of school by the nuns."

"How narrow-minded of them!"

"They didn't see each other for so long. Long after the memory of the scandal was forgotten. Then Dorothy ran into Kathleen, saw she had kids, and gave her a broad hint. 'Wouldn't it be too bad if your kids found out the truth about their background?'"

"Blackmail," said Scorch. "This has real potential."

"Yeah, well, blackmail's on the back burner for now. Worse things are turning up. Lover boy told Kathleen about our contract. That's how come she tossed him out."

"Did she believe he sold his soul? Is that why?"

"No! That's the thing; she thinks we don't exist. And let's keep it that way. But Larry's a chronic liar. She thinks it's all another one of his lies and can't take any more."

"Ah! So where do you go from there? Think you might try to possess Dorothy?"

Roach had thought about it. He was still wary about an actual possession. He did not relish the thought of being inside Dorothy and under Larry. Besides, he'd paid such poor attention in those mandatory antiexorcism classes.

"Maybe," he replied. "But there's nothing like a little lust to spice things up, as a side dish. I have other plans to get Dorothy into Hell."

"Seems she's raring to go."

"She can sing, that I'll grant her. Not a bad voice at all. I've heard a few better. Only she has a way too high opinion of it. Nothing like a little pride to finish the job. Ever see that TV program, *Sing! Sing! Sing!*?"

"I saw it once. Don't you call in and vote for the one you think is best? I thought it was stupid."

"I'm thinking maybe I can get her on that show and totally ruin her. I got plans."

"Now you're talking. See, Roach, you still got it. Now, you and I both know this setup isn't forever. Someday, you'll be back in Hell. But before you are, there's still a lot of damage you can do. I want you to know I got faith in you."

"Thanks, Scorch. That means a lot to me."

There came a loud blast, and the wart on Scorch's nose lit up red. "Scorch here. What's wrong now?" he said, pressing it. Roach could hear the screechy voice of Satan's receptionist. "What do you mean, where the hell am I? I'm someplace, all right? What does he want now? All right, already! I'll be there! Tell him I'm on my way!" Scorch cut off the call.

"You know who that was," he told Roach.

"Yeah, I guess so."

"You keep up the bad work," Scorch told him, then vanished into a puff of smoke that blew out the window.

19

Larry Kavanaugh wept, as he often did.

He had been told so many times: big boys don't cry, and grown men certainly don't. Yet if he was trying to manipulate someone else and not succeeding, there was nothing quite like a torrent of tears as a last resort.

It usually worked. That last time with Kathleen, it didn't. All she said was, "Oh, stuff it, Larry. I'm sick of it," and walked out on his performance.

This time, he wept from a combination of joy and self-pity. Joy, because he was sharing the circular bed in the bridal suite at the Ritz with Dorothy. (For which Dorothy was paying, which made him much more joyful.) Their passion had broken his sofa bed. It did not matter.

They were at the Ritz because Dorothy was having work done on her house, to give it a whole new look. Gone were her images of Jesus, Mary, and St. Theresa of the Roses. She had even thrown out her poster-size aborted fetuses. The single bed she'd had since childhood would be replaced by a California king. A wall was being knocked out to accommodate it.

Her modest tub was giving way to an enormous Jacuzzi. A bidet was being added. Plumbing costs soared beyond belief. Dorothy was picking up the bill for all of it. Some thought she was turning the cell of a nun into Belle Watling's bordello from *Gone with the Wind*. Dorothy did not care. She had found her soul mate in Larry Kavanaugh. He deserved the best.

Nothing else mattered, only their love. Of course, it helped that she had rescued him from that dreadful Kathleen.

In the midst of such joy, self-pity was there. He wept as he told Dorothy of how spiteful Kathleen truly was, how she made him suffer.

"She's got that sister of hers in the house," he sobbed. "Grace is a man-hating lesbian. Plus Grace is wrecking the place. She's got about a hundred cats in there with her."

"Oh, my poor darling!" Dorothy held him and rocked him like a baby. "My sweetums," she crooned. "Everything will be all right from now on. Don't you worry about a thing!"

Next week, Dorothy had an audition for *Sing! Sing! Sing!* Of course, she had to pass that, then get through the first levels. So many were eliminated. But if she were the winner, if she got that recording contract, there would be no limit to what she could give her precious Larry.

20

S plit Tree Circle had come back to life. The neighbors were no longer
frightened about going outside. Word came down from the medical
examiner. Floyd Ferguson died of an aneurism. The cause was listed as
natural, not homicide.

"I feel better too," Kathleen told Grace. "You know, for a while, I
had the oddest headache. Like someone was trying to push something
cold and slimy into the back of my head. I was going to ask you about
that. But it's gone."

Grace looked astounded. "I felt the same thing. And all of a sudden,
it just went away."

The Ferguson house was a boarded-up eyesore, but that was better
than an active crime scene. Someday, it would be torn down, then
replaced by something far larger and more expensive. A family would
move in. Few would recall what took place there. Someday, but not yet.

"Here's what I can't figure out," Grace told her sister about Dr.
Whitney's report. "Why were the doors and windows shut? Why was
the heat up so high? All it says is 'unknown' as to why the deceased
behaved in this manner."

"So, they think he did that himself?" Kathleen asked.

"Apparently so. There was no evidence that anyone else was in the
house with him."

"Which is no proof that no one was, just that no evidence ever
turned up."

Grace nodded. "That about sums it up. With no evidence, officially,
it didn't happen."

"I hope the worst is over now. Those kids, bad enough their parents

are getting a divorce. They don't need a murder mystery on top of that."
Kathleen sighed. "Thank God for Dante and Virgil."

"Those cats are the greatest. And a lot of the kids' friends have
divorced parents too. So, they know it's not the end of the world."

"Sometimes I think the end of the world is if their parents stay
together."

Grace nodded. "You hear anything from Larry?"

"Yes. He called. And you know what he was freaking out about?"

"What? The fact that his children live a few doors away from what
looked like a violent crime?"

"Guess again!"

"Why, I can't imagine!"

"He was worried because he's still part-owner of this house. And
that having a murder so close by reduced his property values."

"Doggone, I should have known!"

"Oh. One other thing. Our friend, Mr. Stink Bug? Turns out that's
not his real name after all. It's Johnny LaRoche."

"Johnny LaRoche. Sounds like some guy who plays the piano in
a sleazy lounge. Johnny LaRoche, appearing nightly. Now, isn't that
special?"

Kathleen laughed. "Larry and his imaginary friend! But I've been
hearing stories about what Larry's been up to since he left."

"What's being said?"

"That he's got a not-so-imaginary friend. He's having an affair."

"Do tell!"

"That's all I know. Someone said, someone said, it's like my favorite
Norman Rockwell painting: *Gossip*."

"I thought you liked *The Plumbers* best."

"It's a tie."

"Whatever, that story started someplace. Where do you think?"

"Apparently someone saw him leaving the Round Robin with a
floozy."

"He didn't waste much time, did he? Who might this floozy be?"

"That, I don't know. But I'm having Pit Bull check it out."

"If that's in the least bit true, Pit Bull is going to kill him in court.

And if he thinks he can get even joint custody of those kids, he's got another think coming. It's like he's determined to self-destruct."

"And I'm not going to interrupt him. Only this time I'm not going to pick up the pieces when he does."

21

A pleasant evening had settled in. Kathleen was alone on the front porch, enjoying the new peace and quiet. Inside, she was hoping it was not the calm before another storm.

I'm different now, she told herself. *Not afraid all the time, like I was before. And the kids don't have to walk on eggs, so afraid that Larry will yell at them. If this business at the Ferguson house happened while Larry was still here, I would have had a nervous breakdown by now.*

She could hear Grace inside, reading the kids a bedtime story. Now, as a rule, Bobby and Jeanine were far too sophisticated for a bedtime story. However, this was one of Grace's specialties.

"They're getting a great scientific education," Grace decided, "but it would be nice to let them know more about literature and art."

Kathleen's mind wandered back a few years. Larry, as a rule, did not do bedtime stories. "Too busy, too tired." But on that one occasion …

She had been driving them back from a New Year's party. Larry was in no condition to drive. He thought he was only a bit buzzed, but Kathleen would not trust him with the keys. "Suit yourself," he finally said and slithered into the back seat.

"I've been thinking," he said on the way home. "About my New Year's resolution."

"And which one was that?"

"My mind's made up. I'm gonna be a better dad to my kids. Yeah. I'm gonna coach Bobby's soccer team."

"Bobby plays lacrosse, not soccer."

"Yeah? I'll go to Jeanine's dance recital."

"Jeanine's not in the dance troupe. She's in Mathletes."

"Yeah, whatever. I'll give 'em lots of attention, lots of um, positive feedback. And I'm starting now. Gonna make up for lost time, read 'em a bedtime story."

"Larry, it's after midnight. They're sound asleep!"

"I'm gonna read 'em a bedtime story, and that's that!"

When they got home, he did. "Wake 'em up!" he insisted. The children were confused and frightened; still, he read out loud to them from *Curious George* till he passed out on the floor.

Kathleen felt a pang of shame that she had subjected her children to such behavior. But Larry was all about Larry, and she had given in to him again. By dawn, his New Year's resolution was forgotten, and his head was pounding.

But that was then. Kathleen listened to what Grace was reading to the children and the cats that had them so spellbound.

"Now I'm sure you know that there are some grown-ups who break the promises they made when they got married," Grace began.

"Oh, yeah," said Bobby.

"That's on all the soap operas," Jeanine added.

Kathleen thought, *In real life too.*

"This is a story of what happens to them. Now, can you imagine a place where the wind blows so hard you can't stand up to it? It picks you up and carries you away?"

"There really is such a place," said Jeanine. "I know because I had to do a report on it. It's called Exoplanet HD 189733b."

"Not in this solar system," Bobby said.

"No, silly! That's why it's Exoplanet. It's in the constellation Vulpecula. Sixty-three light-years away."

"Wow."

"Bigger wow: the wind speeds go up to 5,400 miles per hour. Which is also the Fahrenheit temperature."

"Hardly seems possible."

"Well, it is," Jeanine replied to him. "It's a real place."

Kathleen thought of Larry and his floozy, exiled to Exoplanet HD 189733b. It was a cheerful thought. But no, Larry was probably going to end up someplace worse. After all, he said he was under contract.

"Jeanine, I'm so glad you did that report," Grace said. "Because it is a real place, and here is what happened when the real Dante and Virgil paid a visit to a place just like Exoplanet HD 189733b. Only they called it the second circle of Inferno.

"Now, in Italy during the Middle Ages, you were not supposed to get married because you were in love. Your parents picked out the person you were supposed to marry. There was a beautiful young woman named Francesca, and she was married to a crabby old man named Giovanni. Now this Giovanni had a much younger brother named Paolo. He was really good-looking, nothing like Giovanni. He, too, was married to someone else. Paolo and Francesca were spending a lot of time together."

"I bet they fell in love," Jeanine said.

"I bet they didn't," Bobby said. "Why should they?"

"They did," Grace explained. "They were in love for years. Then one day, they were reading all this romance stuff. They got carried away. And who should walk in on them but Giovanni? He was so jealous he murdered them both."

"Wow," said Jeanine. "That's sad."

"Real sad that they ended up in this Inferno," said Bobby.

"Dante thought so too, so when he and Virgil saw her and Paolo, he asked her what had become of them. She told them she and Paolo had been reading a romance book but didn't read all of it."

"They should have kept reading, to see what happened," Jeanine said. "I would have."

"Well, they didn't. And because they let themselves get swept away, they ended up in a place where they'd be swept away forever. Just like the Exoplanet. Dante was so sad to hear it that he fainted, and Virgil had to pick him up."

"Gee," said Bobby. "Were there any other people in that place?"

"Quite a few. Helen of Troy," said Grace. "Cleopatra. Dido."

"Who's Dido?" Bobby asked.

"She was the queen of a place called Carthage. You will meet her in one of Virgil's stories."

Grace then started to recite "Canto 5" of the *Inferno*, pausing often for questions and comments. Kathleen went back inside as dusk fell and the streetlights went on.

She tried to imagine what it was like, a place where the wind blew at 5,400 miles per hour. Simply beyond her imagination. Yet Dante had come up with it so many centuries ago.

Jeanine said, "It's a real place."

It was hardly the sort of place anyone would care to visit. The fact that it was sixty-three light-years away did not make it any less real.

A real place.

That night, Kathleen managed to sleep without the help of a pill. But she dreamed of Larry, in the den, signing a contract with a man who looked and acted like a normal person. But was not. In the background, Jeanine was saying, "It's a real place, Mom, just like Dante and Virgil said. It's a real place."

It's real. Even though you can't see or touch it. Or it's in another dimension. Or sixty-three light-years away. Or you can't imagine it. It's real, Mom.

It's real.

22

Scorch was running out of patience. He had spent what felt like an eternity in his lab, trying to figure out why the connector malfunctioned.

According to his data, the connector was supposed to burrow into the mind of the primary and then implant a virus in a secondary. The more a primary hated a secondary, the stronger the bond would be, the more information it would yield. Which it did!

Scorch analyzed his background notes. Roach's primary was Dorothy Marie Walsh. Since her childhood, she had hated Kathleen McGrath Kavanaugh and her sister, Grace McGrath. She even had the goods on Kathleen and was thinking about blackmailing her. According to his data flow, Kathleen and Grace had been infected with the virus as planned.

Then, snap, crackle, pop. The connection broke off. It was as if something inside both sisters cured the virus and broke the connection.

How in the hell did that happen? It was flat-out impossible! This whole connector upgrade was new, but in the trial phase, Scorch had never seen such a thing happen.

He began running scenarios, inserting variables. In every one, the virus in a secondary functioned flawlessly.

Something was missing here, and Scorch knew that he'd damn well better find it before Satan found out that he had a system failure in his talons. It was going to be a long night.

Meanwhile, in the Upper World, Roach decided to complete a task that had gone undone since he was waylaid by Floyd Ferguson. He'd return to Split Tree Circle to check up on what was going on, since that connector was not feeding him any data from Kathleen.

Again, he waited till after dark. Disguised as another average young man, he crept though the park to Split Tree Circle. Few lights were on, and the Kavanaugh house was as dark as the Ferguson house.

There should have been some sort of passage here, established by Scorch's connector. There was absolutely nothing.

Since Roach could not access the inside of the house through the connector, he'd have to risk going in without that layer of protection. Which would be difficult. But not impossible. Larry Kavanaugh was still the part-owner of the house, and he had invited Roach inside. Could that get him through the front door?

It did.

The only source of light came from the streetlight outside, so Roach had to wait to let his eyes adapt. There was a bookcase with a large potted plant on top. He heard a scampering sound. It could not be an animal, since there were none when he was here before.

He looked around the living room. There ahead was the den where the deed was done. He took a step forward and banged his knee on the coffee table. Before he could utter an expletive, he saw a large book.

It was *The Divine Comedy*.

Unable to sustain his disguise any longer, he reverted to his true form. His fists clenched with rage. His teeth clenched, his faced turned crimson, and he blasted a stench of brimstone from beneath his tail.

Suddenly, he heard a serpentine hissing. On top of the bookcase, beside the potted plant, there were four points of light. Cat eyes! Two of them, and they were snarling at him, their fur standing out straight.

He must destroy them both, then every other living thing in this house. He lunged for the brown one, who was too quick. He then went after the white one, his maw open all the way, about to crush it in his jaws. But the white cat heaved the plant into his mouth, and his fangs snapped shut on dirt. Roach tried to scream, but dirt poured down his throat and clogged his cry.

"Dante! Virgil! What's going on?" came a voice from upstairs. Roach vanished through a window and did not stop running till he was safely back in his own den. He was still gagging on the dirt.

"Sis? What is it?" said Kathleen.

"Oh, for gosh sakes, nothing," said Grace. "The cats knocked that plant over. I'll clean it up."

"Never mind. After all those cats have done for us, we can overlook a few of their hijinks."

The light went off, and again, all was silence.

23

ScorchIT@inferno.org: Roach? You there, bro?

(no reply)

ScorchIT@inferno.org: Roach? This is urgent!

(no reply)

ScorchIT@inferno.org: Where the hell did you go? I need to talk to you right now!

(no reply)

ScorchIT@inferno.org: Look, bro, I got a flaw in the connector. At least the one I gave you. We have several thousand of these in the Upper World, and if I can't figure out where the flaw is, we might have to do a recall on all of them. You know what our asshole of a boss is going to do to me if we have a recall?

Roach@hellraiser.com: ai ... ai ... ai ...

ScorchIT@inferno.org: You're not making any sense!

Roach@hellraiser.com: They attacked me!

ScorchIT@inferno.org: Who attacked you?

Roach@hellraiser.com: ai ... ai ... ai ...

ScorchIT@inferno.org: Roach, in the name of all that's unholy, who attacked you? Was it an exorcist? Talk to me!

(no reply)

ScorchIT@inferno.org: Those bounty hunters? Did they get you? Roach!

(no reply)

ScorchIT@inferno.org: Roach! Answer me! Was it Michael?

Roach@hellraiser.com: ai ... ai ... no, no, no!

S corch swore loudly. He had to assume Roach was still in the Upper World as opposed to a holding cell in Hell. But Roach's wart was long gone, so there was no way of fast tracking him. He sent one more message.

ScorchIT@inferno.org: I'm coming to get you, because if we don't figure this out before Old Scratch gets wise …
Roach@hellraiser.com: I could have been a contender.
ScorchIT@inferno.org: FUBAR!

In return, all Scorch got were repetitions. "I could have been a contender" over and over again. The signal showed the coordinates of Roach's den. It was better than nothing.

ScorchIT@inferno.org: Roach! Keep the channel open—you hear me?
Roach@hellraiser.com: I could have been a contender.

"I should have known, when Roach went rogue, it was not going to end well. And if I get blamed for a major product recall, I won't either."

Scorch logged off all his devices in the lab, in case Satan should stop in, access his files, and learn how bad the situation was. Should Satan call, he'd get a recording that IT was temporarily unavailable. "Leave your name and number. We will be back to you as soon as possible." Scorch could only hope it never came to that.

24

Dorothy's audition for *Sing! Sing! Sing!* was indeed a challenge. None of the big-time star power judges were present at this stage. But she understood: this was only to eliminate those whose ambitions far exceeded their talent.

"Ms. Walsh? We are ready for you now."

Dorothy's palms were damp from nervousness. She had seen other contestants, once finished, come out. Some were looking smug, assuming that of course they made the first level. Others (told "Don't call us, we'll call you") came out mad. "How dare he tell me to rethink my entire career! Why, in high school, I was Laurey in *Oklahoma!*"

Dorothy's mind reached out for her guardian angel. Odd, he did not seem to be there. It would be comforting to feel his presence.

"You're not nervous, are you?" the judge asked.

"Oh, no!"

"Well, don't be. Just relax."

He sounded like Larry.

"Now, Ms. Walsh, you sing in the soprano range. Is that correct?"

"I do."

"Very well. Here is what we would like you to do. And this is a test of a true soprano. Your voice hasn't been warmed up yet today, correct?"

"No, I have not done any practice since last night, like you said."

"Perfect. We want you to sing the national anthem. But not from the top. We want you to start with the rocket's red glare. All the way to the end. Think you can handle that, from a cold start?"

"I'll try," she said.

"Just say when."

Dorothy cleared her throat, said when, took a deep breath, and reached for that high note. She hit it spot-on and went on to the home of the brave.

"Woo!" said one of the judges. "She's got those bombs bursting in air, all right!"

The poker-faced judge said only, "Thank you, Ms. Walsh. Next, please?"

Of course, it would be a while before the winners got notified. That was her thought during the long drive home. That and being able to share it with Larry. But there was another notion that gave her far more satisfaction.

She had a fantasy about Kathleen or Grace McGrath turning on the TV. And there she would be.

Take that!

And let's say she did not wash out on the first level. They'd be glued to that screen, week after week, thinking of how they once conspired to destroy her. Oh, how sorry they would be!

And if she won, it would be such a tasty revenge.

Tonight, there would be dinner at a posh steakhouse with Larry. Then back to her newly remodeled house for another night of unbridled joy.

Larry had promised he'd be pleased, whatever the audition results were. Oh, he was such a dear man, Larry was. Kathleen certainly did not deserve him. He had his quirks. If she did not return a call or text right away, he'd get jealous.

"Where were you?"

"Who were you with?"

"Why did it take you so long?"

No doubt he was insecure.

Dorothy would cure him of that. He could be sure of her love, even when she was a star and he was still nothing more than Larry Kavanaugh. And if that wasn't true love, nothing was.

25

"Roach! Roach! Wake up, dammit!"

Roach was halfway on his sofa, halfway on the floor, with his tail under the rug. The stench of brimstone filled his apartment. Scorch gave him a hard slap.

"I said to wake up!"

"Aaaiii." Roach sighed.

"Who did this to you? Roach?"

Scorch was ready to panic. If Roach did not come to, what was he supposed to do? Call 911? For a demon? Or carry him back to Hell, where there was still a warrant out for his arrest?

Roach moaned.

"Talk to me, bro!" Scorch begged him. "If we don't get this connector thing fixed, Satan's going to mop up the Highway to Hell with me. Now, come on!"

"Scorch?"

"Yes, it's me! Scorch! And I need your help, now!"

"I made a mistake, was wrong to even try …"

"What are you jabbering about? You mean the fact you went rogue?"

"No," Roach groaned. "We were both wrong … so long ago … before time began … we had a chance to sign on with Michael. We should have …"

Scorch hit him a lot harder. "Don't you dare say that! Don't you dare even think that! We are demons, you hear me? Proud demons! Never, ever forget that!"

Roach drooled. "Look at you!" Scorch mocked him. "What a mess, a once proud demon! Who or what did this to you? Can you at least tell me that?"

Roach shook his head and mumbled, "Caaaats."

"What? Cats?"

"Caaaats."

"You mean lions and tigers?"

"Noooo. Caaaats."

Roach opened his mouth, and a mound of dirt dropped out.

"You are really disgusting, you know that?"

"Scorch. I need mouthwash. I need toothpaste. But if I brushed my teeth forever, I couldn't get rid of the taste of that dirt." Roach wept.

"All right!" said Scorch. "You want me to go to that CVS and get you toothpaste? Is that it? What brand would you like? The one that makes you sexy?" he snarled.

"No, no, no …"

"Then just tell me what happened, in as few words as possible. Because I need your help, Roach, big-time."

"Last night. I went to the Kavanaugh house. I wanted to see why the connector I had on Kathleen went kaput."

"Yes. And? How did you get in?"

"It's where I signed the contract with that fool. He asked me inside. Still valid, so I went right through the door."

"Then what happened?"

"Then. It was dark. I walked into the coffee table, and, and, and, there it was …" Roach let out a wail of anguish. "There it was!"

"There was what? Cats?"

"That book!"

"What book? What could it be that got you into this condition?"

"That book, Scorch! Dante's book!"

"*The Divine Comedy*?"

Roach let out a high-pitched keen.

"I could have been in it, Scorch! I could have been the star of the whole thing, but Old Scratch wouldn't let me talk to Dante or Virgil! Wouldn't even let me near them! Said I wasn't evil enough!" Roach broke down into sobs. "I could have been the biggest, meanest demon in Western classical literature. I had my spiel all prepared in Italian, in *terza rima*. Oh, it was so unfair!"

"Um, Roach?" Scorch asked. Roach looked up at this friend with swollen red eyes.

"Don't you think you're carrying this obsession with *The Divine Comedy* a bit too far? It's been, what? Seven hundred years? You weren't in *Rosemary's Baby* either. So what is the big deal here?"

"We're talking about the biggest and the best!"

"Oooo-kay," said Scorch. "Now, what happened with the cats?"

"They attacked me."

"And they were what? Big jungle cats? The ones that ate Christians in the Colosseum? Back in the good old days when our pal Nero was large and in charge?"

"No. Just house cats. Little cats."

"I tried to warn you about that, didn't I? What did I tell you about children and animals?"

But Roach broke down into sobs again. "Just cats. I was so mad I was going to kill them. Then kill everybody else in that house. Then blow it up. But one of them, the white one, threw a plant right in my mouth. Dirt and all. And somebody called those damn cats … Dante and Virgil!" Roach was heaving with sobs.

Scorch groaned. "All right," he said. "I can see how you might have a problem. With two cats. Named Dante and Virgil. But we have a much more urgent problem staring at us right now, and not seven hundred years ago. You follow me?"

Roach nodded.

"So focus! You said you got in that house to try to find out what happened to the connector from your sweet little Dorothy to Kathleen. For starts, tell me—what did you find?"

"Nothing! The connector was gone. Only it must have been there because it did give me some data. Before it snapped."

"Nothing at all? No little bits of it on another plane of reality?"

"I didn't have a chance to look."

Scorch gave him the look that said, *Fat lot of help you are.*

"I'm sorry, Scorch!"

"Yeah, well, we don't have time for you to be sorry. Because I was in the lab, running every possible scenario. And it works! In the lab. But not in the real world. And if I don't figure out why, and it happens again, and you know who finds out, need I say more?"

"I'm so sorry, Scorch."

"Sorry don't cut it. Hmmm. I could go over there myself."

"But you can't get in, since you're a demon, and no one in the house ever gave you consent to come in."

"Big problem."

"Maybe you can ring the bell and say you're a Jehovah's Witness?" Roach suggested. "Or we could disguise ourselves as a pair of Mormon missionaries?"

"Very funny," said Scorch. "Ha, ha, ha."

"There are two kids in that house. Kathleen and that sister of hers are going to be damn careful about who gets in."

"I could be a meter reader," Scorch said.

"From what I've seen, nobody uses indoor meters anymore."

Scorch muttered a slang term for excrement. "I'll have to think about this," he said, "and I don't want you to go back there by yourself. Too dangerous. But let me ask this. Is the connector link between yourself and Dorothy still active?"

Roach checked his tablet and muttered the same slang term. "Not only is it alive, I've got a ton of messages from her. Seems she went through with the audition for *Sing! Sing! Sing!* Without me! I sure hope she didn't blow it!"

"I'd say that's the least of our worries. Gimme that." Scorch ran a test on the tablet. No apparent defect at all. He ran a report.

"I'm going back to the lab with this," Scorch said, "and see if there's any hidden flaw in the bond you have with Dorothy. That could explain it. Meanwhile, you lie low. And for once, try to stay out of trouble."

Roach fell back on the sofa and started in again: "I could have been a contender."

26

Grace arrived back on Split Tree Circle after her day shift at the hospital. "Sis! I'm home."

"Meow! Meow!"

"Hey, guys, I'm home!"

"And I'm glad of it," said Kathleen. "I need to show you something before Bobby and Jeanine get back."

"Sure, what is it? Oh, hey, I'm sorry about your plant."

"Don't worry about it. Accidents happen. But there's something else here, and I don't want the kids to know about it. Yet. It could be nothing. But I don't want to put them through any more trouble. They've had enough."

"What could it possibly be?" Grace noticed that the door of Larry's den was shut.

"Come in the den. Now, do you notice anything weird?"

"Besides the fact that this is Larry's inner sanctum? Now that you mention it, yes. It's colder in here than in the rest of the house. Not so much cold but dank. Like a nasty rainy day. Makes you eager to leave."

"It's not my imagination then. But look at this."

Kathleen got out the laser pointer. "Watch Dante and Virgil."

The cats chased the dot all over the living room. Once it was in the den, they refused to follow it inside.

"Oh wow. That's like *Twilight Zone.*"

Kathleen left the den door shut. "That chill has been in there awhile. Since before Larry left. But the way the cats reacted really troubled me."

"Meow! Meow!"

"It's like they're trying to tell us something. They just don't have the words."

"Grace, this might sound silly, but do you believe in evil?"

"In my work, how can I not? I see great evil, all the time, in what people do to other people. Especially to those they claim to love. And to themselves."

"Now, I'm not saying that Larry Kavanaugh and truth belong in the same sentence. And this notion of his selling his soul to the devil is beyond the beyond. But he said the deed was done in that den. At his rolltop desk.

"With some demon acting as the devil's rep. LaRoche, Larry said his name was. Johnny LaRoche.

"And now I'm starting to wonder if any part of that could be true. Do I sound like a complete fool? Or as if Larry has finally driven me over the edge?"

"No, you don't. Now as you know, at the hospital, we do get patients who claim diabolic intervention. Or outright possession. And I must admit, I don't think I've ever seen a case in which that turned out to be the only possible diagnosis."

"Have you ever called an exorcist for a patient?"

"Not me, personally. But I've heard stories from credible sources. Now, this was not on my shift. But there was a teenage girl who sent naked selfies to her boyfriend. He shared them all over the place. She tried to poison herself. There was some talk of a demonic influence. What became of her, I don't know. But it's always been my opinion to look for a natural cause before anything supernatural."

"You know, with Larry, what worried me the most? That he'd gone in debt to a loan shark and missed a payment."

"Which would endanger not only Larry but you and Bobby and Jeanine."

"Not that he was thinking about anybody but himself. However, if he was in fact dealing with a live demon in there …"

"Okay," said Grace. "Here's what I recommend."

"You and four out of five doctors, at least."

"I'd say, go for all five. First, we need to eliminate any natural causes. Is the furnace in good shape?"

"As far as I know."

"That's step one. Have it inspected. Another thing: it could be a clogged heating duct leading to the den. Have you ever had those ducts cleaned?"

"El Cheapo never got around to it."

"We are about to. Now, what's directly over that den?"

"Bobby's room."

"What's under it? Storage?"

"Crawl space."

"Yes, and wasn't it me who thought Floyd Ferguson had a dead animal in his own crawl space? Did I ever call that one wrong! But there could be something down there. We need to call Leo's Trapping. He's humane. If there is something down there, he'll relocate it, not kill it."

"Good for Leo, but I hate to think of what might be lurking down there."

"Probably just the usual spiders and snakes."

"Yuck."

"We'll have Leo take some pictures. We need proof of what's going on. It may be that whatever is spooking the cats is in the crawl space."

"And suppose we do all that, and the problems don't go away? What then?"

"Then I'm going to discreetly consult with Father Flynn at St. Teresa of Kolkata. We're hardly at the point of needing an exorcist, but a quiet little house blessing just might be in order. He's done this sort of thing before. No harm in it."

"I hope it doesn't go that far."

From outside came: "Mom! Aunt Grace! We're home!"

"We're in here," said Kathleen.

"Discussing the state of the world with Dante and Virgil. I was just telling your mom why I have always loved cats. Did you know that their beautiful eyes can see in the dark? Yes, indeed, and some say they can see into other dimensions. You think so?"

27

Scorch, hard at work in his lab, was getting nowhere fast. He was not taking calls. There had been two so far about his connector. It worked fine for a primary victim, but as for the virus that was supposed to infect the secondary, that had failed twice. Once in South Africa, the other in Siberia. So, what was going on?

Scorch had left a recording, advising both demons to turn the whole connector off, then turn it back on.

Meanwhile, he had his prototype set up. Again, he ran every variable. "A demon implants this thing into the mind of the primary. The connector goes through the memories of the primary, isolating persons whom the primary hates. Then infects those secondaries with a virus, which gives the demon access to their memories. And it works fine, here! What seems to be the problem?"

Scorch knew he needed to start thinking outside the box. "Hate is what we want. Hate is the most powerful destructive force. We have only had two, no, make that three failures. Out of thousands. So far. Dammit, there were not supposed to be any!"

Scorch analyzed the pattern at hand. The primary, Dorothy Walsh, was nursing a grudge for Kathleen McGrath since they were both children. Dorothy was blaming the McGrath sisters for the fact that she was denied a chance to render ... "The Good Ship Lollipop" ... hmmm. The secondary connection with Grace was weak anyway. Not that important. But the Kathleen/Dorothy connection could not have been stronger. The young Dorothy was afraid that Kathleen and her sister conspired to ruin her singing career. Afraid, yes.

"Now Kathleen and her sister, from what little data we obtained from her, had a traumatic experience involving an older brother who committed a violent crime. Who had some sort of mental defect. And as a result, Kathleen grew up with a phobia of mentally ill people. No matter if they were severely insane or slightly eccentric. Therefore, she married that idiot Larry, thinking he would protect her. From what she feared. Then suddenly the secondary connection Roach had with her went into full failure mode.

"Because … because …"

Scorch felt a chill in his hot lab. "Because why does anyone hate anyone? Because they are afraid! That's it! They see the other … the hated other … as having power over them, so the hate comes out of fear. Hate is only the mask that fear wears."

Slowly, Roach set up the prototype again, using the Dorothy/Kathleen connection. Instead of hate, he inserted the variable of fear. He pressed the start button. The secondary connection functioned without flaw.

Until Kathleen got so disgusted with Larry, she threw him out of the house. She did not need his protection, because she rejected her fear. Said no to it! Threw it out the window with all of Larry's junk.

At that point, the secondary connection snapped like a wooden toothpick. Shattered. Useless.

Scorch shouted out a demonic word that was a combination of *Eureka!* And *Oh shit!*

28

The work was done, quickly and quietly. Nothing at all was wrong with the furnace. As for the duct work, Bobby marveled at the volume of dust bunnies that came out. All Leo found was a nest of nonpoisonous snakes, which he removed. His pictures showed nothing out of the ordinary, just a creepy crawl space.

Still, the chill remained in the den, and the cats would not go in. Grace's friend Father Flynn agreed that a house blessing certainly would not hurt. He had to ask her and Kathleen a few questions in advance.

"Have there been any poltergeist phenomena, objects moving without being touched?" he asked.

"No, nothing that we're aware of. There used to be a large plant on top of that bookcase, but we're sure the cats knocked it over."

"I see. Any other manifestations?"

"The den is a lot colder than the other rooms. It should not be; everything's been checked out. And the cats still refuse to go in there," Grace replied.

"But that's where my ex said the deed was done," Kathleen added.

"Tell me what he alleged happened in there."

"He said he signed a contract with the devil in exchange for his soul," Kathleen explained. "Well, not the actual devil but a demon claiming to be the devil's agent."

"An agent. I see."

"And, well, Larry's always been dishonest, but that was so outlandish I just could not take any more of it."

"I follow you. And I'm not saying that actually took place. But what

I must tell you is, if it did, such an entity such as this demon cannot enter a home unless it is invited."

"Larry asked it in?"

"Or it could not come in. Is there anyone else in this house who might have invited this creature inside?"

"We have two minor children. Impossible."

"I'm not saying this to alarm you. And there is no sign that you need a full exorcism. But what Larry appears to have done is issue a standing invitation to an unclean spirit. If he really is a demon, he is invisible in his natural form. Unless the invitation is rescinded, this demon is able to enter this house any time he pleases."

Dante and Virgil meowed.

"The way your cats have been acting, and the temperature drop in the den, may well be indicators of its having been here."

"I don't believe this!" said Kathleen. "No, Father, I do believe what you are saying. But that Larry would be so irresponsible as to invite a demon in here? A demon? From Hell? Into a home where his children live?"

"I've never had much faith in Larry," Grace added, "but it seems to me what he's done now is fool around with something way beyond himself."

"No wonder he was being so secretive! I should have tossed him out long ago. But I was afraid, and I shouldn't have been. I should have been strong. For Bobby and Jeanine."

Father Flynn went ahead with the house blessing. That evening, the temperature in the den climbed back to normal. Bobby and Jeanine had Dante and Virgil chasing the red dot around the rolltop desk.

29

That night, Roach decided to pay another call at the Kavanaugh house. Never mind what Scorch told him to do. Stay out of trouble? Who did Scorch think he was to give advice like that? From what he was hearing, Scorch was in a lot more trouble than he was.

At least some of the heat was off Roach. It was now safe to drift about in his invisible form. Old Scratch had called off the bounty hunters. They were more needed for a situation in the Middle East.

Besides, Satan was livid about the connector failure and recall. He stormed around Hell, shrieking that he never wanted to hear the words *new and improved* again. Scorch might be in the torture chamber for a while. But Hell's IT department could not last long without bad old Scorch.

This time, those cats would not be any problem. They'd be dead. Then he'd really show the McGrath sisters something they'd never forget. Of course, he'd be invisible, but he'd shatter everything breakable in that house. Send it flying! Then he'd make his natural form visible to those kids. They'd never stop screaming. He'd kill off Bobby. Jeanine, he'd keep for a little fun.

Here was Split Tree Circle. He walked right up to the door to drift though it as he had before. *Boink!*

What the hell was this? The door was a solid barrier to him. But why? Didn't Larry Kavanaugh give consent for him to walk right in? Never said he couldn't.

He tried again. *Boink!* Ow!

How ironic that he was standing on a mat that said: Welcome! With no secondary bond to Kathleen, there was no way in. What a stinker that Larry Kavanaugh was, to cancel his invitation without saying anything! He'd pay.

Roach swore, then thought about where he would go next. There was one place where no one would pull a cheap trick like that on him. He'd go see Dorothy. Yes, he had some happy news from Dorothy. She'd been called from the Hollywood headquarters of *Sing! Sing! Sing!* There was none of this don't call us, we'll call you. They called her! They wanted her to appear in the first level. Dorothy had picked out her song: "I Will Always Love You."

The idea of her singing it with Larry Kavanaugh in mind was sickening. It was only a step in a much larger plan to bring her and that creep boyfriend of hers down. Sometimes you just had to make a little sacrifice when the end justified the means.

Dorothy and Larry were not in when Roach arrived. However, someone was around. Roach noticed a strange car parked at the end of the street. Inside was a man with a camera, equipped with a telephoto lens. He, too, must be waiting for the lovers.

Roach drifted into the house. This was his first good look at it since the remodeling had been finished. He liked the new look a lot better than the old one. It was garish beyond belief. "Who redecorated this place?" Roach asked himself. "Say, Liberace?" There were gold satin sheets on the bed of one who had once been a consecrated virgin.

Then he heard a car pull up into the driveway and drifted to the top of the roof. He'd wait here till Dorothy and Larry finished their business, and he could creep back into her dormant mind. He heard them talking.

"I don't see why you had to go all the way to Pine Grove," Larry was saying.

"It was nothing, darling. Give me a kiss."

Unknown to them, the photographer up the street was clicking away as they prolonged their kiss.

Larry finally spoke. "You can walk to the CVS here, so why go all that way?"

"Darling, really. It was nothing of any importance."

"But I like having my widdle snookums handy."

"Now oo-ums got your widdle snookums wight here." There came the sound of passionate kissing and several more clicks.

Hurry up, you fool. I've got to access her mind, Roach thought to Larry.

Even as a demon, Roach was revolted by the sounds from the bedroom. He turned his fine hearing to the stranger in the car, who was dialing his phone.

"Yo, Pit Bull?" he said. "Got it. Date and time-stamped, like you said. You online now? Here it comes." Then the man hung up and drove off into the night.

Roach had to grin. This night was not going to be a total waste, as he had feared. He waited till the bedroom was silent, then drifted back inside. Both of the lovers were conked out and naked: not a pretty sight. Roach used to connector to get into Dorothy's mind.

She was so excited! Yes, next week, she would be flying out to Hollywood to appear live on *Sing! Sing! Sing!* She had her outfit all picked out. Larry, of course, was coming with her. "He gets concerned when he's away from me. And jealous."

Roach deduced that Larry must have no sense at all but did not convey the thought.

"'I Will Always Love You.' You remember—Whitney Houston sang it? Dolly Parton wrote it. Of course, Larry's worried about all this expense."

Because he is a cheap bastard.

"How very nice. You are going to win that level, Dorothy. I know it." He felt like the first witch in *Macbeth*. *You will win!*

The second-level witch would say: *You will win!*

One more witch would say: *You will put on the performance of your life, dearie.*

"You have done so much for me! I can't say how much!"

"There will be more, dearest Dorothy. Much more. Sweet dreams."

Before drifting away, Roach did a quick scan deep inside Dorothy. What was this? Another complication, which could work very much to his advantage. Was Dorothy aware of it? On a certain level, which she was not yet prepared to handle.

"That's right," he told her. "Be a good girl and dream on. All will be well. Just leave everything to me."

30

I t wasn't easy for Grace to say nothing to her sister. But she did not
want to disclose this information in front of the children. They knew
nothing of Dorothy. How fortunate they were. So, Grace waited till
they were safely out of earshot before telling her sister: "You would not
believe the latest about Dorothy Walsh!"

"I do believe it, sis. I already know it. I should have known something
like this would happen."

"You know it! I nearly fell over when I heard it!"

"Wait ... you already knew? That means I really am the last to
know?"

"That she's going to be on *Sing! Sing! Sing!* next week?"

"You have got to be kidding! No, I meant that she's the one Larry's
having the affair with."

"Oh, no way, Jose! You're serious, right?"

"Serious as an earthquake. Dorothy's the one. Pit Bull's got proof.
Yep, I should have seen this coming. Whatever. As she is about to learn,
he's no prize. But what's this about her being on TV?"

"Okay. This is what one of the other nurses told me. She goes to St.
Catherine's, in Sodality, very active. Now, according to her, Dorothy
auditioned, did so well she got picked for the first level next week."

"Dorothy's actually doing this?"

"Next week! Live! But it seems there's a lot more going on. Most
at St. Catherine's are praying that she'll win. That she'll go on to the
second round. But some are worrying about her. She's rarely if ever at
Mass. She's neglecting her duties as the head of the pro-life committee.
And she had work done at her house. A big remodel job. They're

wondering, how is she going to pay for it all on her salary? She hasn't tried to contact you about that, has she?"

"If she thinks I'm paying for the mess she made, she's in for a big surprise."

"She's acting weird. Not like herself at all. They are wondering if she's having some sort of nervous breakdown. Now, my friend did not say anything about her having an affair, but there has been some speculation. She's been spotted in some nasty places. Dressing in the sort of style she used to complain about. Skirt up to here, neckline down to there."

"At her age? She must look ridiculous."

"I think I heard once that after Mother Superior kicked her out of the convent, she became a consecrated virgin."

"I'm sure Larry put an end to that."

Grace got out a bottle of Mommy's Time-Out. "I propose a toast! To Dorothy! May she put on a show that will never be forgotten as millions applaud!"

Kathleen agreed. "I'll drink to that!"

"Doesn't this make everything so much better?"

Kathleen leaned back on the sofa. "It is better around here, you know? Ever since that visit from your friend, Father Flynn. It seems the kids are more at ease, a lot less sniping between the two of them."

"As are the cats."

"I mean, I just don't know. Larry is so full of it. Did he, in fact, bring an evil spirit into this house?"

"Would you put it past him?"

"No, but every time I thought he could not get worse, he did. An affair with Dorothy. Doesn't that top everything?"

"No, bringing an evil spirit into his own home has to be the top. But you're right, sis. The vibes in this house are different—a lot different— since the blessing was done. It feels like a real home now, a safe place."

"I've been thinking about so many things. What Larry says he did, is it even possible? It seems to me that there are levels of reality. Other dimensions. All around us."

"How do you mean?"

"I was walking down the sidewalk yesterday. And I saw an ant walking in the other direction. And I'm aware of myself walking. And I'm aware of the ant. He must have some awareness of himself, but does he have even the slightest concept of me? How far does his consciousness go? And my own?"

"I think what you're saying is there are many levels of reality, and the fact that we can't comprehend them does not make them any the less real."

"Think about this. Seven hundred years ago, there was a poet named Dante."

"Meow?"

"Yes. Just like you," Kathleen said, inviting him into her lap. "He was writing a poem set in Hell. How can he even imagine such a place? Is it possible that he got into another dimension and projected himself to a planet sixty-three light-years away? And used that as his inspiration for his Second Circle of Inferno?"

"Very possible. Dante was a genius, and that's what it takes to open up your mind to the realities most people can't even imagine. Speaking of which, how are the kids doing in school?"

"Always good, but now they're doing even better since their so-called father isn't around to yell at them all the time. Bobby still hasn't made up his mind, but he's kind of leaning toward a medical career."

"Give him time. He's seven."

"Jeanine has her mind made up. She was an astrophysicist long before she could say the word."

"Great little girl."

Grace refilled their glasses. "Ever notice that the more we swallow of this, the more enlightened we are?"

"Here's to our enlightenment! But if it turns out that Larry really did bring something evil into this house ..."

"It's gone now," Grace said.

"That clammy feeling in the den. The way the cats refused to go in. Now I understand those can be symptoms of something very wrong. And even if that thing, which I'm uncomfortable in naming—"

"It might come back and say, 'You rang?'"

"Yes! Even if it's, thank God, out of this house now, some of the things going on make me wonder."

"If it's really back in Hell, where it belongs?"

"What happened to Floyd Ferguson and that girl in the ER who tried to poison herself. Didn't somebody say something about diabolical intervention?"

"Well, no proof of any such thing ever came up."

"But think about this, sis. This Dorothy business. Not that I'd care to go near her, but it's said that she's not acting like herself."

"Having an affair with a soon-to-be-divorced man certainly doesn't sound like Dorothy."

"No. It sounds like something else is in the driver's seat inside Dorothy's head."

"Are you talking about an actual possession?"

"Do you think that might be it?"

"Well, sis, an actual possession has clear symptoms. Above and beyond the green vomit, of course. Is Dorothy suddenly fluent in a language she's never heard? Can she levitate? Does she have the physical strength of Popeye on spinach? I'm not hearing any of that. What I am hearing is out-of-character, highly irresponsible behavior on her part. Having an affair, going deeply into debt, appearing on *Sing! Sing! Sing!* may be symptoms of poor judgment. Possibly of some sort of mental breakdown. But not anywhere near a state of possession."

"So maybe this thing is back in Hell and will leave us alone."

"I'll drink to that," said Grace, "though perhaps I've had enough."

"Grace, do you think we should watch the show?"

"Oh, I'm all for that! If you want!"

"Ordinarily, I don't watch that sort of thing. It's been a while since I last saw *Sing! Sing! Sing!* I thought it was pretty silly. All flashing lights and colors to distract you from the fact that many of these contestants can't sing at all. Plus these guest hosts call themselves celebrities. Most of them, I've never heard of."

"You know, I have not seen Dorothy since she got expelled. I may have heard her sing a few times, a little-girl screech. And I would not want to go near her now. Even though I don't look like I'm still in kindergarten. Still, she might remember me and get all mean again. No, I don't want that. But I'm curious. Do you suppose she can actually sing?"

"She never was one of those child divas on PBS."

"Yeah, all too often they burn out their voices before they grow up."

"So maybe we saved Dorothy from that, and she ought to thank us for spoiling her career when we did."

Grace hiccupped. "Oops, I really have had enough. But let's do it! Wednesday night at eight. Oh, and one other thing. Remind me to stop by the liquor store for more Mommy's Time-Out."

"We'll never make it through the Dorothy Hour without it!"

31

Larry was not around. George, his own lawyer, had called him and said they had to get together on this divorce business. Some evidence had turned up. "This is not good! No, it cannot wait! It's urgent!"

Dorothy once asked him why he needed George. "Isn't he just an extra expense? After all, you are an attorney."

Larry hemmed and hawed and said, "There's an old saying, darling. Any attorney who represents himself has a fool for a client." He chose not to tell her what George was up against: Pit Bull. The mere thought of facing Pit Bull in a courtroom weakened his bladder.

In a sense, Dorothy felt relief. Her boudoir was a shambles of half-packed suitcases in preparation for their trip to Hollywood. But Larry was getting so possessive, so clingy, needing to know where she was all the time. It could be tiresome. Not that she didn't love him, she did, but she needed to room to breathe. Larry was starting to suffocate her.

She sat down on her chaise lounge and had to think. There was no sensation of her guardian angel being around. Just as well; for once, there was something she needed to do alone.

Last night, she had the strangest dream after her angel went away. She dreamed about her beloved mother, five years dead. Mom was trying to speak: *Stop, stop, stop, Dorothy.* It was as if Mom was still feeling the effects of her last stroke; she was fighting to form words.

Get this man. Out of bed. Out of house. Out of life. Sold self. Evil.

Then the dream became more nebulous. Someone else was whispering so faintly to her.

My name is Moira Elizabeth. Just like your mom. When you see my face, you will see her and not miss her so much.

"Who are you?" Dorothy asked, but the odd little voice was gone.

Whatever! There was something she needed done, and she'd better do it now, while Larry was still downtown, before she lost her nerve.

In her new bathroom, she reached under the vanity stand and pulled out the plastic bag from the CVS in Pine Grove. As Larry reminded her, she could well have purchased this at the CVS nearby, but she did not want to do so where someone might know her.

With shaking fingers, she pulled out the Maybe Baby Home Pregnancy Test. She read the directions. Any fool could understand how to use this. Her hands trembled as she tried not to make too much of a mess.

Then she left it on the vanity top, sat on the rim of her new Jacuzzi, and waited. And waited. And was pleased that Larry's legal business was taking way too long.

"Time's up!"

Slowly she picked it up to see the results.

Positive. *Yes, you are!*

A wave of shock passed over her. How could this have happened? *How do you think?*

Dorothy destroyed the kit and the directions and stuffed them into the trash can at the curb. The trash men would come in the morning. Larry would not know until she chose to tell him.

"And I will tell him, yes, once we're back from Hollywood," she decided. "He will be so thrilled. He has to be! But, maybe it will work out for the best if I don't win."

Larry was home shortly thereafter. He looked troubled.

"Honey, I'm afraid there's bad news. George says he does not want me to go to Hollywood with you."

"But, darling, it's all set up. I've got our plane tickets, hotel reservations, and you have a reserved front-row seat!"

"That's just it! You know how on *Sing! Sing! Sing!* the camera sweeps over the audience? Especially those in the best seats! He says millions of people could see me there. And George feels that for the time being, you and I should not be seen in public together. You can't get more public than that."

"Oh dear, I'll be all by myself. And I'm supposed to do 'And I Will Always Love You'! You won't be there to hear me."

"I will hear you, all right, on TV. And I'll be with you in spirit. Your number one fan, egging you right to the top, where you belong."

That night as Larry snored beside her, Dorothy wept. Then she felt her guardian angel's presence.

"I'm so disappointed. I wanted Larry to be with me," she sobbed.

"My little songbird. Never mind about Larry. He can survive a little while without you. Even if he thinks he can't. But I'll be up on that stage with you, Dorothy. I will get you through it. And I have everything under control."

32

The McGrath sisters had their battle plan laid out for Wednesday night. Kathleen decided to tell the children something she thought she'd never say to them.

"I was in second grade, and Grace was in kindergarten. There was a girl in my class named Dorothy. She was very mean to both of us. We were both going through a hard time, and she would not stop picking on us."

"Was she a bully?" Bobby asked.

"That's putting it mildly," Grace told him.

"So, what happened to her?" Jeanine had to know.

"The principal of our school expelled her."

Jeanine turned to Bobby. "That means she got thrown out."

"Yeah, I figured that. Did she keep bothering you after that?"

"No, she wasn't even allowed on school property. So, no more bullying. But as it happens, Dorothy thought she was a terrific singer. And she was supposed to have a big role in the spring recital. Then the whole recital had to be cancelled."

"Because she got thrown out," Jeanine said.

"Yes, and there were a lot of bad feelings. Of course, Dorothy blamed us, not just for the end of the recital but for spoiling what she thought was going to be a big career."

"Sounds like a brass-plated spoiled brat," Jeanine decided.

"You called that right," Grace added.

"But now she's back. Sort of," Kathleen went on. "You know that program *Sing! Sing! Sing!*?"

"Yeah, but we're not supposed to watch it because it's on a school night," Jeanine offered.

"And it's silly," Bobby added.

"Sometimes it's silly," Kathleen said. "A few of the contestants really can sing well."

"Once in a while," said Grace.

"Anyhow, this Dorothy is going to be on the first level on Wednesday night, so Grace and I will be watching."

"To see if she messes up and laugh at her?" Bobby asked.

"That's the thing," said Grace. "We haven't heard her sing since we were your age. Is she really that good? We want to find out."

"May we watch it? Even if we have school the next day?" Jeanine asked. "I just want to see what she looks like, Mom."

"Well ..." It occurred to Kathleen that Jeanine had a good idea, in case Dorothy ever tried to approach the children. They would know to run the other way. "Okay, just the part where she sings. We'll call you when it's Dorothy's turn."

"It's a deal!"

"And one other thing," Grace added. "You know how it works? You're supposed to text or tweet in the one you like best? Let's have all our electronics ready. Just in case."

The countdown proceeded. Grace had purchased a fan magazine that explained how the whole thing worked. *Sing! Sing! Sing!* was performed live on the second Wednesday of each month.

"Okay, you have a panel of three real recording artists. From the first level, they pick fifteen for the second level. They have to count all the texts and tweets."

"The rest get tossed out, right?" Jeanine asked.

"You got it. Now those fifteen will compete in the second round, which picks ten finalists. The third round picks out the winner. He or she wins a recording contract. Fame, fortune, what have you."

"You think Dorothy's going to get that far?" Bobby asked.

"When pigs fly," said Grace. "No, I really don't see how she can survive the first round, but again, we just don't know."

"We can't know how her voice changed as she grew up. We don't know what she's capable of doing."

"We sort of know," Grace said.

"Who's on this session's panel?" Jeanine asked.

"Let's see. First, Jared Winters."

"I must say, I never heard of him," Kathleen said.

"I have!" Jeanine said. "I really like him a lot! He's so cute!"

"He's so cuuuute!" Bobby added.

"Please!" Grace cautioned him. "He must be the resident teen heartthrob. Next, LaShawn Curry. Didn't she have a big hit last year?"

"One that got a lot of the stuffed shirts mad at her," said Kathleen. "But she's got guts. I like her."

"Me too," said Grace. "The last one? Lord, have mercy, this is the iconic one."

"For Pete's sake, who is it?"

"Longianna Rae."

The children both said, "Wow!"

"I've got some of her CDs," Jeanine added.

"And I have a whole bunch of them. I'll bring them over, so we can see what Dorothy's dealing with."

"I think it's safe to make a bet," Kathleen offered. "If Dorothy's testing herself with Longianna Rae, she has all the chances of a snowball in Hell."

"You're on!" said Grace. "I say, if she makes second round, you owe me an extra bottle of Mommy's Time-Out!"

The sisters shook on it. The countdown went on.

33

Johnny LaRoche and Kumar were back, this time prowling the corridors of Los Angeles International Airport. Kumar was slightly worse for wear.

"Old Scratch had me hanging upside down for three days in the Emperor Nero aula, while everything still in Hell threw sewage at me. Even the damned souls. I hate him."

"Not as much as I do," said Johnny LaRoche.

"I guess it could have been worse, since so many other demons are still tied up in Mosul. Still, there's a principle here."

"But Old Scratch did let you go after three days?"

"He did. And said not to screw the pooch like that again. The asshole."

"Well, screw him. I've got a full agenda. What did you say Dorothy's flight number was?"

"Two thirty-eight. And according to the board, it's running on time."

"Look over there."

Roach spotted a limo driver from *Sing! Sing! Sing!* holding up a sign that said: Dorothy M. Walsh.

"Lover boy won't be with her?" Scorch asked.

"Nope. His lawyer said not to be seen with her anymore. *Her* lawyer got the goods on this little fling they're having. So, he's charging Larry with adultery, which means the divorce is a done deal, and lover boy loses his shirt over it."

"He already lost his shorts over Dorothy, so why not?"

Roach had to snicker. An announcement came over the PA: "Attention. Flight 238, now arriving at gate E7."

"Come on," said Roach. "Let's watch."

Hidden in the crowd, they saw Dorothy get off, go to her driver, then pick up a vast quantity of luggage from the carousel. Then they were gone.

"What did Olivia Neutron Bomb remind us? The wheels are in motion," Roach told his old battle buddy.

"Yeah, but, you know, I have to get back to Hell. Are you going to be all right with this? Do you need anything from down below?"

"Not that I can think of right now."

"Have you thought about doing a full possession on her yet?" Scorch asked, knowing it would be Roach's first and most high risk.

"It's still under consideration," said Roach.

He had devoted a lot more thought to it than he was letting on. The only thing holding him back was the notion of being with Larry Kavanaugh. That was too far beneath his dignity.

"Things are working out in my favor. A lot better than our jerk of a boss will ever believe."

Johnny then vanished onto an airport bus. Kumar vanished into thin air. No one noticed or cared.

34

Zero minus three days and counting. All systems go.

Jeanine and Bobby were watching a program on PBS, which had been taped in Milan. There was Longianna Rae singing a duet with the Italian tenor, Gianni Corvoni. Jeanine and Bobby called him Opera Dude. It was *Gattara*, Cat Lady, one of her own songs, her latest chart topper.

"What's it about?" Bobby asked.

"Well, see, there's this old lady in Rome. Where there's lots of feral cats. That means the poor cats don't have homes. But this old lady feeds and takes care of them."

"That's nice of her."

"But she's got secret powers, see? If you were ever in love with somebody else and had to leave them, but now you have to get in contact with them, the old cat lady can find them for you."

"No way!" said Bobby.

"Yes way," said Jeanine. "Opera Dude is a VIP. But he's dying. And he asks the cat lady to tell his girlfriend. Even though they haven't seen each other in fifty years."

"And?"

"And the cat lady finds her and tells her! Then they sing together for a while, she tells him she always loved him. Then he dies. Get it?"

"Wow." Bobby thought about that for a while.

"You'd think Longianna Rae and Opera Dude were really in love with each other," Jeanine offered her opinion.

"But they're not," said Bobby. "Longianna Rae and Opera Dude are real good friends, but they're not in love."

"And how would you know, Mr. Smart Guy?"

"He's gay. It's a well-known fact. His husband's a flight attendant for Alitalia."

"You sure know a lot of useless information, you know that?"

"I take great pride in my knowledge."

Longianna Rae sang that "Rome's cats and kittens dance with glee, when she comes to their colony, our lady of the cats is she, the one they call Gattara."

Corvoni took up the refrain: "Gattara, set my spirit free, I had a love not meant to be, does my love still remember me, will you find her, Gattara?"

In Milan, they were given an ovation. From Grace on the sofa, they got "Mama Mia!"

"You are going to lose, sis," Kathleen warned her. "Dorothy needs her head examined if she thinks she can hold a candle to that."

"We'll just see about it," Grace told her. "Be prepared to pay up. Just in case. And Jeanine and Bobby, remember what I said."

"Have all the phones charged up just before the show begins. We didn't forget!" Then they ran out with the cats.

"Here are Longianna's CDs," Grace told her sister. "The first one is *Forever*, and here's some of her later stuff. But, seriously, what can go wrong?"

Kathleen said, "Dorothy wins. That's the worst thing. If she's really unstable, winning can be worse than losing."

35

Zero minus twenty minutes and counting. Roach was in his invisible form, so no one saw him lurking high above the set of *Sing! Sing! Sing!*

Sound and light checks were in progress. The audience was filling up the seats. One of the technicians was placed in front, so Larry's seat would not show up as vacant when the camera swept the fans.

"Here they come," Roach muttered. "An African American screech queen. A teenybopper's first sexual fantasy. And Longianna Rae." Roach ground his teeth and spat. "The boss can't stand Longianna Rae. Then he takes it out on us. I ought to haul off and clobber her for all the trouble she's caused."

Zero minus fifteen. Grace went down her list. Liquid refreshment for Mommy and Auntie Grace? Heh, heh. Check! Electronics charged? Check! Chips and dip? Check! Root beer for the kiddies? Check! Cat Snax for Dante and Virgil? Check!

Bobby and Jeanine managed to wheedle their mother into letting them watch the whole show, not just Dorothy's part. Grace covered the table with a special-occasion cloth while singing softly to herself: "Rome's cats and kittens dance with glee, when she comes to their colony, our lady of the cats is she, the one they call Gattara."

Zero minus ten. Larry was alone, house-sitting for Dorothy. Which he resented so greatly. It was more like house arrest. He was a man. He was an attorney. Since he had spoken those words so often, he came to believe them. He had a man's needs. Which no one ever satisfied better than Dorothy. And yet here he was, turning into a gofer for little miss superstar. He didn't like it and secretly hoped she'd lose tonight.

Larry contemplated what his own attorney had lectured him on: the need to be a lot more discreet. "Not only can you not afford to be seen on TV with her, you must take more care not to flaunt your relationship. Never leave your car in her driveway again. In fact, keep it off her block. There's a big shopping center close by. Best to park it there. Another thing: if her landline rings while you are in her house, whatever you do, don't answer it. Let the machine take a message."

Speaking of which: *Ring! Ring!*

Larry reached for the phone, then drew his hand back. "No one is here to take your call right now," Dorothy's voice said. "Please leave your name and number, and we'll get back to you as soon as we can."

We. What did she think this place was, the Vatican?

There was a click, and a male voice spoke. "Ms. Walsh? This is Patrick the plumber. Two things. First, I want to let you know that Ann and I are tuned in. We'll be rooting for you tonight! Second, about that payment you mailed to us last week. It's still not here. Since it was for such a large amount, I wanted to make you aware, so you might want to consult with your bank and stop payment on it. So, give me a call when you're back from LA. Best of luck!" (Click.)

Larry stared at the phone, scratched his head, and asked himself, "What the hell?"

He'd been bringing in her mail, like a star's good little gofer. Much of it was junk, but there were a lot of envelopes from other contractors who had worked on the remodeling. What was going on here? Some financial irregularities? Larry began to wonder, just how well did he know Dorothy?

He decided to get her letter opener, use it to open the flaps of some bills, then glue them back shut. Maybe it was all nothing. A harmless misunderstanding.

The TV in the living room shouted: "Stay tuned for *Sing! Sing! Sing!* after these messages!"

"Yeah, after the program's done and so is Dorothy," Larry promised himself.

There was a burst of flashing multicolored lights and theme music. "Welcome, America! Welcome to another session of *Sing! Sing! Sing!*

And are we going to sing our hearts out tonight! We've got you twenty of the best!"

(Loud applause.)

"Let's welcome our celebrity guest hosts! Here he is, the artist who has just released the smash hit 'Bubbles of Love,' from Denver, Colorado, Jared Winters!"

(Much high-pitched female screaming. Jeanine joined in.)

Kathleen turned to Grace. "He's an artist?" she asked.

"Do what the nuns said. Take it on faith. Have a drink."

"And now, let's have a big hand for the artist who's got 'Red-Hot Curry' burning up the charts, the singing sensation from Southeast DC, LaShawn Curry!"

(Whoops and applause.)

LaShawn waved to her fans. She was exquisite in her matching kente cloth dress and head wrap.

"And now, Ladies and Gentlemen, a real classic! Her latest release is topping the charts in the good old USA, and Italy, and yes, I'm talking about *Gattara!* Cat Lady! Here she is, from Los Angeles! Will you welcome Longianna Rae!"

The place went wild. Longianna had to take several bows and keep repeating, "Thank you. Thank you. *Grazie mille!*" It was a while before the audience let her be seated.

"She sparkles," said Jeanine.

All Bobby could add was "Wow!"

"You're a bit young for her," was Grace's advice.

Far above, Roach bared his teeth and snarled. He wanted to tear her limb from limb. He had to remind himself: *Focus.*

Contestants were chosen at random. The first was a cowboy from Wyoming, who rendered a sad tale of ruined romance, dead hound dogs, and wrecked four-by-fours.

"He's all right," Grace pronounced.

"He'll do, if you're into red state misery."

Numbers on the bottom of the screen showed how to text and tweet to vote for this contestant. Longianna Rae said, "You're sincere, and I can appreciate that."

"Damned with faint praise."

The next contestant was a massively obese young man from New Jersey. His version of Sinatra's "When Somebody Loves You" showed a perfect balance of power and sweetness.

"He'll be in the finals. I just know," was Grace's opinion.

"Are we going to tweet yet?" Bobby asked.

"Let's see Dorothy first."

Dorothy was number 3. When she walked up on the stage, the ladies of St. Catherine's Sodality gasped to see how little she was wearing.

"Dorothy Walsh, welcome!" said the emcee. "And what are you going to sing for us tonight?"

Roach sprang to attention. He sent her a thought. "I'm with you Dorothy. Leave everything to me. Now tell that fool what you are going to sing!"

"'I Will Always Love You.'"

"Take it away, Dorothy!"

The McGrath sisters sprang to the edge of the sofa.

Dorothy went to the center of the stage, locking eyes with the technician in Larry's seat. She began softly, singing to Larry that she must leave, that all she had left were bittersweet memories. Then she took a deep breath.

The sisters looked at each other. "Not bad! Not bad at all!"

That's when Roach took her out of time. She was no longer on stage but walking in the park with a little girl in a calico sundress. The child had Dorothy's mother's bright blue eyes, fair, freckled skin, and unruly red hair. "My name is Moira Elizabeth. I love you, Mommy!"

Then Dorothy was back on the stage. She paused for less than a second.

"And I will always love you!"

Her voice was like an ember that exploded into a blaze. The studio shook with the force of it. The audience was shrieking. All three guest hosts were blown away.

"What did we just hear? Bobby! Jeanine! Start tweeting!" Grace shouted.

"But we thought she was nasty."

"Never mind that," Kathleen said. "Tweet! Now!"

Larry, who had just popped open a can of beer, poured it into his lap.

"Dorothy, that was fantastic!" Longianna Rae told her. "Thank you so much for letting us hear it! You must love someone very much!"

"Oh, yes, I do," she said.

Far above, Roach took a bow to acknowledge the applause. "Thank you, Ladies and Gentlemen! And for my next number …"

His eyes glowed red when he thought of what that would be. "The fun has only started."

At the end of the evening, the finalists were announced. They were the obese guy, Dorothy, and a few more the McGrath sisters could not even remember.

"A toast!" said Grace. "To our old archenemy. I never knew she had it in her. Did you?"

36

Larry sat, stunned, in a puddle of beer.

He knew Dorothy sang. She told him so, many times. He had even heard her singing in the shower. However, he had not been interested in her singing. Dorothy was for something else.

From what little he had heard with the shower running, she was all right. He had no idea she could deliver a performance like that.

And now she was going on to the second level. Larry finally rose and tried to sop up the mess with a whole roll of paper towels. The living room still reeked of beer.

Larry could not sleep. The landline rang and rang. Finally, the recording changed to: "We are out of memory and can take no more messages. Please call back."

We. Again.

Then he reminded himself: "Oh, yeah. These bills. Quickie look."

He needed Dorothy's letter opener and a glue stick to seal them back up. The glue stick was on top of her desk. He could not find the letter opener, so he looked in the drawer, and there it was. He pulled it out, with a letter.

The letter reeked of April in Paris and was addressed to Kathleen. The dainty handwriting was clearly Dorothy's.

What the hell was this? Larry did not know that there was ever a connection between Dorothy and his wife. Where could they possibly have met each other? Were they friends? Enemies? Long-lost kin? Lesbian ex-lovers? What?

Kathleen had always been so damn secretive. When they started dating, her father was long dead. Her mother couldn't stand Larry.

Grace wasn't wild about him either. There was so little he knew about the McGrath family backstory. Was Dorothy somehow a part of it? Why, then, didn't Kathleen ever talk about Dorothy?

Slowly and carefully, he placed the letter opener under the flap and pulled out the sheet of paper.

> Furthermore, it is my belief that if you refuse to tell them, you are not acting in their best interest. If you then refuse to allow me to speak with them, I will understand, but I will require an initial payment of $20,000, cash, in small bills. Kindly place them in a plain brown bag and leave it in the hollow tree by the swing set in the park.

Larry refolded the letter, glued it back into the envelope, and placed it back where he found it. He whistled. "This is blackmail," he whispered to the empty house. "This is big. Huge!"

He then opened and resealed several bills. "Past due. Please remit. Third request. We will take legal action unless ..."

And then there was that call from Patrick the plumber. Did Dorothy ever send him any payment at all?

Dorothy's financial situation was far worse than he thought. Just what was she trying to pull off?

Perhaps she was so sure she'd win *Sing! Sing! Sing!* she presumed it would be easy to cover these costs. "But hell! She hasn't won yet. More sessions to go. Anyone's chances of being the winner are, what? Way worse than one in a million. And if you win, there's no money. You get a recording contract. Then you have to release something that people are going to buy. If it doesn't sell, you are toast. No guarantees."

Larry tried to remember the names of last year's winners. He came up blank.

"So, it seems that Dorothy cooked up an alternate plan. She'd blackmail Kathleen. For what? Or did she? This letter was never sent. Were there others?"

He was getting a headache from stress and the stink of stale beer.

"Whatever," he groaned. "At least I've got this, in case I need leverage against her. Yeah, just in case."

He may have slept till just after dawn. Then the doorbell started ringing. Larry knew better than to answer the bell. He heard objects being left off.

After noon, he peeked outside. There were enough flowers in the yard for a Mafia funeral.

"Superstar can haul them in herself. I'm sick of being her damn maid."

Then he heard a large vehicle pull into the driveway. He looked through the window. It was an airport limo. Dorothy bounced out. As the driver pulled out way too much luggage, a gaggle of teenagers appeared, demanding autographs and selfies with Dorothy. She gladly obliged.

"My adoring public! Gag me," Larry muttered. "Superstar is about to make her grand entrance. Two can play at this game."

"My goodness, look at all of these lovely flowers!" Dorothy let herself in. "People are so kind! Larry? Darling?"

He had run upstairs and curled into a fetal position in their bed. He was unshaven, unshowered, and clad only in dirty, smelly underwear.

"My, my, my! It smells like a barroom in here! Lar-RY!"

He heard the clunks of suitcases being put on the floor. He thought of the scene in *Whatever Happened to Baby Jane?* in which Bette Davis served Joan Crawford a dead rat for lunch.

"Darling? Can you bring these flowers in?"

Hell, no.

"And I'll need a little help in getting the suitcases back upstairs." Dorothy did not dare add, "Because I'm in no condition to do that myself." That must wait. The timing of her big announcement had to be perfect.

Larry heard her on the stairs. *Here it comes.*

"Why, darling, look at you! Sound asleep at this hour! Well, I guess you were up late!"

Larry rubbed his eyes. "I guess I was," he mumbled. "Congratulations."

"Is that all you can think to say?"

"Well, you took 'em all by storm. The unholy Trinity. Including the teenage personal vibrator."

"Don't be such a wet blanket! So many texts, tweets, and those lovely messages on the Facebook page!"

A phrase in Latin, which he learned at Jesuit High, came back to him. He fell back on the pillow. "Sic transit gloria mundi."

"What was that?"

Larry let out a long belch. "It means Gloria threw up on the bus on Monday."

"Apropos of what? Anyhow, darling, I will need your assistance with the flowers. And in getting my luggage upstairs."

My luggage? Why not *our* luggage?

"Larry, be a dear! I have so much I need to tell you. Above all ..."

"Above all!" He belched again. "Above all, if you can equal or top that performance in the next two programs, that makes you winner-winner-chicken-dinner. And where is it going to leave me?"

"Oh, darling!" Roach drifted down from the ceiling and whispered, *Tell him now.*

"My sweet Larry, you mean the world to me. Didn't you know that? You will be rid of Kathleen soon. You will be free."

"Yeah, soon, once Pit Bull takes me to the cleaners."

"Darling, it won't make any difference. You will still mean everything to me. Because, darling, listen to me. I, I mean, we ..."

We. Again.

Dorothy took his head into her hands and whispered into his ear. "We're going to have ..."

Larry jumped up from the bed. "You are going to have a what!"

"A baby, Larry. Our baby, think of it!"

"And are you sure?"

"Yes!"

Larry Kavanaugh collapsed back on the bed, hid his face in his hands, and cried great heaving sobs.

"Larry!"

"No!" he repeated with each sob. "No, no, no!"

Roach drifted up to the roof and snorted with laughter.

37

"It's all over the hospital grapevine," Grace announced during dinner. "Local songbird makes good. But here's what's weird."

"Spill," said Kathleen. Bobby and Jeanine were all ears. So were Dante and Virgil.

"You know how she always had to be the center of attention? Always wanted to be in the school paper?"

"Did she ever!"

"The funny thing is, now, no one in the media seems to be able to get hold of her! Not the local news channel, not any of the papers, not even the newsletter from St. Catherine's. You think she'd be dying for the free publicity. But it seems she's in her house, not answering the phone or doorbell. That's not like her at all."

"I heard something," Jeanine said.

"And what was that?"

"That she doesn't feel well. She caught some kind of virus on the airplane home."

"That's odd," said Kathleen. "I saw her on Channel 8, getting off the plane, like she was the queen of Sheba or something, still with that grin on her face."

"I got mine. Too bad about yours," Grace said.

"Just saying. She looked great. Not sick at all."

"Could be," Grace admitted. "Still, in this business, you have to keep the momentum going. Like a snowball, keep rolling it so it gets bigger. And it looks like Dorothy is dropping that snowball."

"The public is fickle. I read that someplace," Bobby observed.

"You're right, Bobby," said his mother. "If you don't keep reminding people, they will forget about you. Especially now, Dorothy needs as much publicity as she can get."

"Well, there are still lots more levels. It's not time for Nasty Dorothy to dance in the end zone. Not yet," Bobby noted.

"You're very observant," his mother said. "How did you come up with that?"

"I was reading that the next level will be NFL night. The Baltimore Ravens are going to be there."

"All of them?" Grace asked. "Woo!"

"Quite a few."

"What was it that Greta Garbo used to say?" Grace asked. "I vant to be alone?"

"Greta Garbo was a big enough star that she could risk that. Dorothy's just starting out," Kathleen told her. "It's one of these things; sick or well, you have to deal with your fans."

"And when you don't," said Grace, "they're not your fans anymore. This is not like Dorothy. Something is afoot here, and darned if I can figure it out."

38

Larry looked up at Dorothy, still unwashed, unshaven, with swollen red eyes. "No," was all he said.

"You can't mean that! Our baby. Our love, come to life."

"Who told you about the baby?"

"Why, no one. I used the Maybe Baby Home Pregnancy Test."

"Is that supposed to be reliable?"

"It's supposed to be the best."

"It was positive? Where is the damn thing? Let me see it."

"I ... I'm not sure."

"Then how far along are you?"

"Not very. A few weeks, at most."

"Few weeks. Good. We got plenty of time to solve the problem. But we have to act fast."

"*Larry!* This is not a problem; it's a baby. You can't mean what I think you mean. Not that. It's the worst sin a woman can commit."

"You should have thought about that a long time ago. No, Dorothy. I've got enough kids. More than enough. Those two are bleeding me dry. I will not have any more."

"Suppose our baby is like Bobby and Jeanine? You know, gifted?"

"Worse. They cost way too much. I am sick of that sky-high Greenleaf tuition, sick of even thinking what college and grad school are going to cost. And when will it ever pay off? When I'm old. Or dead. No way, Dorothy. You should have at least asked me before you got yourself knocked up."

"Larry, please! All right, I won't ask you for child support. But I'm not going to solve a problem, as you put it."

"Then don't, because I won't pay child support. And how much were you going to ask me for? How about twenty thousand dollars in small bills, stuffed in a plain brown bag, left in a hollow tree, for starts?"

Dorothy could not speak. She turned dead white and sank onto her chaise lounge. Then she started crying.

"That's a hell of a letter you wrote to my wife. What's the story here? What did you want Kathleen to pay you for? How is it you know each other? Dorothy?"

Dorothy kept on weeping.

"You know Kathleen and that lezzie sister of hers never did tell me a lot about their background. There were lots of holes in their story. I never heard either one of them mention Jimmy. Or Isaiah. Who are these people, Dorothy? I suspect you know. They're pretty damn important, aren't they? Well? Aren't they?"

Dorothy finally spoke. "I'm so sorry. I never should have written that down. I was so wrong."

"I bet it was a good idea at the time, right?"

"I'm so sorry!"

"Did you ever extort any money from Kathleen?"

"No, Larry, I swear—I never did!"

"But you thought about it, didn't you?"

Dorothy could only nod.

"All right," Larry said, "all right. We'll forget the whole thing. On one condition. You solve this problem of yours. You solve it once and for all. Or this becomes a matter of public record. They say all publicity is good. But, Dorothy, you and I both know that's not always true. Do you want those teenyboppers out on the sidewalk to know that their singing role model is a felon?"

Dorothy shook her head.

"I knew you'd see things my way. But we have to act fast, because you need to be back on your feet again for the second level. There's a place over on Twelfth Street."

"Oh, Larry, no!" It was the very place where Dorothy once stood outside, holding her plastic fetus and shouting at young women going inside.

"Don't kill your baby!"

Larry thought for a moment. "You're right," he admitted. "Too many people there know you. The probably have your picture in their rogues' gallery. We'll go to the one in Pine Grove. I'll get George to make an appointment in the morning. Dorothy? It's that, or I spill the beans on you. Is that clear? And don't think any of your big shot Hollywood pals can get you out of this."

She nodded. If only her guardian angel were here to help her.

Roach did come to her in the night. "Dearest Dorothy, I totally understand." He did not add that he had heard every word and had nearly laughed his head off. And he hated to be in agreement with a sap like Larry Kavanaugh.

"But Larry has your own best interests at heart. He cares about you. And he wants your career to be a big success. Having a child now would be the worst mistake you could ever make. Don't worry, dear. I'll be with you in Pine Grove. And everything will work out for the best. You will see. Have faith in me. I care."

Dorothy felt herself drifting off into another reality. As if none of this were really happening. She was watching it happen to someone else.

Roach then sent an update to Scorch, who found the whole thing uproariously funny.

"So, what's next?" he laughed. "Little Miss Right to Life is gonna get an abortion. How can you top that?"

"I can, and I will."

"But how? Wait a sec, bro. Are you still thinking about doing a full possession on her?"

"What I'm going to do will make Pazuzu look like a little wimp. When I'm through, that boss of ours will give me a medal. He'll be so damn sorry he kept me out of *The Divine Comedy*. I'll make him kiss me under my tail in the Judas Iscariot aula."

"Oooo-kay," said Scorch, recalling that recently Roach had been walloped by a pair of cats. "If you can pull this off, I'll be cheering the loudest."

"I'm going to put on a show you will never forget."

39

George set everything up. That was the big advantage of being a real attorney, as opposed to a fake. George had moaned, "Talk about an attorney who has a fool for a client! First, he could have had that proof of adultery giftwrapped for Pit Bull. Then he knocks his girlfriend up! I ought to charge him an extra stupidity fee."

However, the utmost discretion was now needed.

The appointment at the Pine Grove clinic was made for John and Jane Doe. Larry and Dorothy left before dawn for the long drive. That was the best time. No fans were hanging around. They would take Larry's car. They could not see the invisible Roach, riding in the luggage rack.

Both wore disguises. Dorothy had on her movie star shades, a large floppy hat, and a scarf to cover her face. She wore the clothing she used to work in the garden. No one would mistake her for Dorothy Walsh.

Larry, who never wore blue jeans, now had on a pair that belonged to a painter. They were spattered with eggshell white and hunter green. He wore aviator glasses, a tattered hoodie, and his Make America Great Again cap.

Once they got onto the interstate, Larry became nasty. "Twenty thousand dollars in a hollow tree. Ridiculous! That's not real life, Dorothy; that's Nancy Drew, Girl Detective."

Dorothy said nothing but watched the passing signs. Very few cars were on the road at this hour. She didn't say anything. Yet she could feel the comforting presence of her guardian angel. It was as if he were hovering over her.

Larry snapped on the radio. Willie Nelson sang of being on the road again. Larry was silent for the next thirty-odd miles.

Then he asked, "Just who are Jimmy and Isaiah? Still don't want to tell me?"

Dorothy shook her head, no.

"Who can I ask? You think Grace might tell me?"

Dorothy blew here nose into a tissue.

"All right! Clam up! Suit yourself. I'll find out sooner or later. And when I do, what happens is really up to you, Dorothy. You cooperate, and I clam up too. You don't? You give the staff at the Pine Grove clinic any grief? You don't want to think about that, Dorothy."

Twenty more miles of silence. They did not hear Roach, singing along with the radio.

"I've been thinking," said Larry. "Now, it seems to me, you are in a lot of financial trouble,"

Dorothy whispered, "Yes. Larry, I loved you so much. I just wanted to make my home a more pleasant place for you."

"Whatever! You are way over your head in debt. You need a lot of cash, and you need it fast. I see only one way. You are not going to blackmail Kathleen, that's for sure. And we didn't dress up like this to play Bonnie and Clyde. No. So here is what you have to do, Dorothy. You have to win *Sing! Sing! Sing!* Get me? Have to. And when they give you that contract, you have to put out something that sells like hotcakes. You have to be the next Longianna Rae. Think you can do it?"

Dorothy said nothing.

"I know the answer to that, Dorothy. You can. I know you can. Because it's all in your reach right now. You have to grab hold of it. Never let go."

As they drove east toward Pine Grove, the sky lightened.

Dorothy could sense her guardian angel backing up everything Larry said. "I'll be with you all the way," he promised. "We will be as one. We will put on the most spectacular performance ever. Not as you and I but as one. Now be brave."

40

"Oh no!" Larry said as they arrived early for Dorothy's appointment. There was already a picket line of protestors lined up.

Dorothy trembled as she saw the young man leading a chant. She knew him. He had been with her in DC last January. They had been stuck in the lounge at Reagan Airport. All she wanted was to get home after the March for Life. They were forced to wait for the blizzard to stop shrieking and the airport to reopen. She was so tired, and her frozen feet hurt. He was such a zealot for the pro-life movement. She thought he'd never stop talking at her.

"Come on, Dor, ah, Jane honey. Here comes one of the escorts. He'll get us past these idiots."

"Stick with me," the escort said. "Remember—they're not allowed to touch you."

"Let's go," Larry said.

"Yes, John," she agreed.

A howl went up for the protestors. A girl tried to hand literature to Dorothy. "If you do this, you will die horribly of breast cancer! Here is scientific proof!"

"No," the escort firmly said.

"Dude!" a teenage boy called to Larry. "Don't do this! If you love that woman, you have to love the child."

Larry made a gesture to smack him. "Cool it," the escort said to Larry. To the boy, he said, "No violence."

"You are the ones who are being violent! You murder babies!"

The closer they got to the door, the more raucous the crowd got.

They held up images of dismembered fetuses. Several women loudly recited rosaries. Others held signs that said, "I regret my abortion."

Roach drifted from the luggage rack to the roof of the clinic. He fed Dorothy a thought. *"Keep walking. That's right. Don't let them stop you."*

The escort held the door open for them. The young man Dorothy remembered so well spat on the ground. "Stop now!" he shouted. "Baby killer!"

Once inside, with the door closed, most of the noise vanished. The zealot outside had no idea that she was Dorothy Walsh.

Dorothy Walsh had no idea that last night he had boasted that he knew her, and had placed a $500 bet on her.

She looked around the waiting room. To her committee members at St. Catherine's, she had always described the interior of the Twelfth Street facility as an Inquisitional torture chamber. The interior was cold, dark, and gloomy. Fetuses born alive were hacked to death by evil doctors.

This place was nothing like that at all. It was clean and well-lighted. There was tasteful artwork on the walls and well-tended live plants. There was even the latest edition of *People*, with Longianna Rae and Gianni Corvoni on the cover.

The staff could not be more kind. "Have a seat in our waiting room, Mr. Doe. Would you like anything? Coffee?"

"Um, sure. Cream and sugar."

Dorothy went into the interview area. "We see that your husband's attorney has provided all the needed paperwork. This form verifies your pregnancy. And I see that your understanding of the HIPPA regulations is in order. Everything here is held in the strictest confidence."

"Yes," said Dorothy.

"Now there is one more question we need to ask you before we go ahead with your procedure. We are a pro-choice facility. And we take that seriously. So, what I'm going to ask you now is this: are you terminating your pregnancy of your own free will? No one is coercing you to do this?"

You got that right, toots, thought Roach.

"Um, yes, it's my own choice, nobody else's."

"Good. Now if you will step this way, please. First, we'll do a quick check of your vital signs. Then, will you remove all of your clothing and put on this gown? You can hang your things up on this rack."

"Oh, could I keep my sunglasses on? I have a condition. Bright light hurts my eyes. And I'd like to keep my scarf."

"Certainly, Ms. Doe. The doctor will be right in."

On the roof, Roach was licking his chops. What did Scorch tell him? You win a few, you lose a few. Roach was done with losing.

At one time, he had imagined Larry Kavanaugh coming home and finding his house burned to the ground. In the remains would be the mutilated bodies of Kathleen, Grace, and both of those damn cats. Above all, Larry would find charred remains of Bobby and Jeanine. How would he feel then? Not so indifferent to those kids anymore, eh? Roach regretted blowing that chance. But this was almost as good! And here was Larry, being so helpful in the termination of his third child. *Moira Elizabeth, soon to be no more.*

There was a knock at the door. "Come in," Dorothy said. A doctor and nurse entered. The doctor asked, for the final time, "Are you sure of your decision, Ms. Doe?"

"Yes. Totally."

"Then let's proceed. You may feel a little …"

Dorothy could not hear any more. What she felt was like having ten hard cramps at once. "Ai!" she cried out. The nurse held her hand.

"That's it," said the doctor. "All done. Now we take you to the recovery room and let you rest a while."

That nurse still held her hand. "Are you okay?" she asked.

"Was it a boy or a girl?" Dorothy asked.

"There was no way to know. Too early to tell. Nothing but a few cells and some tissue. Can you sit up? Very good. You will have a bit of quiet time, we'll make sure you're ready to travel, and then Mr. Doe can take you back home."

Dorothy closed her eyes and whispered, "It was a girl. Moira Elizabeth."

They did not arrive back home till after dark. Dorothy had not spoken once during the long drive back. She felt as if she were on the roof of the car, watching someone else. Nothing hurt. There was no feeling at all. None of her fans were on the sidewalk. Roach was glad to get off the luggage rack.

"After all, I'm going to be the toast of Hell soon. I'm not a suitcase."

Larry escorted Dorothy in the door and sat her down in the living room. "You've had a long day, sweetums. You need a good rest, and in the morning, you'll feel 100 percent better. Are you bleeding?"

"Just a teensy bit."

Larry helped her to lie down on the couch and covered her up. "Want some tea? Anything to eat?'

"No, thanks."

"Want the TV on?"

"PBS would be nice."

"You got it. Now, I have to get out of this disguise and go out for a little while, to the Exxon station."

Dorothy nodded. Of late, it seemed that she knew things that she could not possibly know. She knew Larry was going to the Exxon station. After that, he was going to the Round Robin.

"And you'll be okay here by yourself?"

"I'll be fine. You go ahead."

PBS was presenting an opera from La Scala in Milan. There was Gianni Corvoni, singing as he buttoned himself into the costume of a circus clown.

Ridi, Pagliaccio, sul tuo amore infranto!
Ridi del duol, che t'avvelena il cor!

An English translation ran along the bottom of the screen. "You are not a man! You are nothing but a clown. Laugh, clown! That's what your fans want. Keep them laughing, although your heart is destroyed."

Sing, sing, sing, Dorothy! Sing for your fans. You are not a woman; you are a plastic idol. Keep them so happy they'll buy whatever you put out. Although your heart is destroyed!

As Gianni Corvoni was shaken with sobs, so was Dorothy Walsh. She fell off the sofa and poured out more tears than she ever thought possible.

"Moira, Moira, Moira!" she cried out. "Dear God, what have I done?"

41

Dorothy woke up around midnight on the floor. Larry was still not back. She was not alone. Someone was on the floor behind her, holding her like Larry used to do, once he was sated.

"My dearest Dorothy," Roach whispered in her ear. "I know, I know how hard all of this has been on you. How badly you were hurt as a child. How much you deserve everything of which you were so unfairly deprived. I know, because I too was so cruelly deprived of what I wanted most."

Roach grasped her tighter as he remembered the decree that he was forbidden to speak with Dante and Virgil. "Don't waste their time," is what Satan said. "What could you possibly have to tell them that's so damn important?"

He had tried his best to destroy the McGrath sisters. Then, to be walloped by a pair of cats! And to hear Grace call the cats by name, Dante and Virgil, had opened up an old wound.

"Soon, Dorothy. Just stay with me, and I will make right the wrongs that were done to both of us. I will raise you up to the place you should have been all along. The whole world will be watching."

"You really are my guardian angel."

"Yes, dearest Dorothy."

"What I did today in Pine Grove …"

"Hush now. Hush, hush. It's over. It's done. Put it behind you where it belongs."

Roach rocked her and made shushing sounds in her ear.

"Guardian angel?"

"Yes, dearest?"

"What is your name? You never did tell me."

"Ah, yes. My name. Can you guess what it really is?"

"Why, I don't know."

"Guess, Dorothy. I'll give you three guesses. No, I'll be more generous and give you six."

"John? George? Paul? Ringo?"

Roach had to laugh. "You're funny. Two more."

"Elvis? Rumpelstiltskin?"

"No, no, no, dearest. I'll tell you something. You will know my name. Yes, and you will speak it out loud for the world to hear. When the time is right. Until then, have faith in me. I will be with you every step of the way. Even unto Hollywood."

Roach sank his talons deeper into her soul. There was no resistance, not with so much dry rot. Dorothy relaxed and gradually fell asleep in her new lover's arms. She felt a great sense of peace and trust. So much that she could not feel that the tongue licking her neck was forked.

Larry came crashing in the door at two in the morning, turned on the lights, and cried out, "Oh shit!" when he saw Dorothy on the floor.

"Honey! What happened?"

"I guess I fell off the sofa."

"Can you stand up? Are you all right? Are you bleeding anymore? Let's see."

He pulled Dorothy up. She smelled the whiskey on his breath. She was not bleeding any more than expected.

"Can you make it upstairs? That's the spirit."

Larry got her out of her clothes, into her nightie, and into bed. "I'll be right here, honey. I was so dumb to leave you alone like that. You need rest."

"I'll be all right." It felt strange that Larry was suddenly so attentive.

"I've worked out a plan," Larry said. "You have to win. And you will. I'll see to it. Now I know it's just more expense, but I'm going to get you a voice coach. Just to be sure you come out on top of the next round. And once you feel up to it, you will be talking with all those reporters who have been trying to get hold of you. I've already put out word that you got sick on the plane back home. A little virus. No big deal. But you are feeling much better now, right?"

"Yes, Larry. Yes, I am, thank you."

Dorothy drifted back to sleep. "Of course he's worried about you," Roach whispered. "You're nothing more to him than a meal ticket. Remember I'm the one who truly loves you."

"I know." She sighed. "I know, whoever you may be."

42

"Sis, can I ask you something?"

"Shoot," said Grace.

"Would it be all right if I went with you to Mass at St. Teresa's next Sunday?"

"You need not ask. Of course! How about Bobby and Jeanine? They want to go?"

"Them too."

"There's plenty of room in my car. I'll get all that good stuff out of the back seat, and off we'll go. Will the eleven o'clock service be good?"

"Fine. I've been thinking. I'd like to thank Father Flynn."

"He'll be there. Don't you worry."

"Things have just perked up so much around here. And I'm not saying I know why. Maybe it was something perfectly natural."

"Like having all that dirt out of the ducts, so the furnace can actually work?"

"Yes. Or getting the snakes out of the crawl space. Yuck."

"They weren't poisonous."

"Still, yuck. I'm no fan of snakes. Or maybe the fact that Larry's not here anymore. I just don't know. Still, I'd like to thank him in person."

"He'd like that fine," Grace agreed.

Kathleen did not have to worry that the children would be squirmy. When Grace introduced them to Father Flynn after Mass, they were on their best behavior.

"Hello, I'm Jeanine."

"And what would you like to be when you grow up, Jeanine?"

"An astrophysicist. Bobby and I go to Greenleaf. I'm thinking about Challenger Memorial for high school. And MIT for college."

"Really, now!"

"Yes, and I have a theory too. Science and religion are not opposing each other. It's like they're different branches of the same tree with the same roots. Just because we don't understand something does not mean isn't real. Oh, here's my brother, Bobby. He's real!"

"How do you do, sir?" Bobby said.

"And you, young man?" What would you like to be?"

"I haven't made up my mind yet. I'm just a kid. But I do like animals, so maybe I'll be a vet. Aunt Grace has two cats. Their names are Dante and Virgil. They're neat. Aunt Grace is reading us stories about the real Dante and Virgil."

"You are reading to them from *The Divine Comedy*?"

"Sure. Just to give them a bit of the humanities."

"And when we're done with that, Aunt Grace is going to read to us about some guy named Aeneas."

"Some guy named Aeneas. Right. Great story. You will love it." To Kathleen he said, "These children are amazing."

"Don't I know it, Father. Look, I want to thank you for all you did for us. The atmosphere in the house is so improved."

"It was my honor, Ms. Kavanaugh. And if there is any problem, you call me about it."

"Will do!"

"If you don't mind," Grace said, "I'd like to ask Father Flynn a question."

"Certainly," he said. "Would you like to come on into the office?"

Once inside, Grace said, "Look, I don't know what was going on in that house. I just can't say for sure. Whatever, the problem seems to be solved."

"Well, that's good."

"But there's something that maybe you can enlighten me about. I haven't really said that much about my sister. Or the kids."

"Both of them, excuse me, just blew my mind."

"They are terrific. Kathleen, well, I guess you understand, was in a bad marriage. It got off to a poor start. Our mother hated Larry. She saw right through him. I never really cared for him. He made up stories about other people that weren't true. That was a big red flag. He's a phony. And once those kids came along ...″

"Any father of children like that ought to be so proud of them."

"Not Larry! To him, they were nothing but a burden. He constantly whined about how much he had to spend on them. And never talked to them except to yell or bark orders. No, it was a relief to them to have Larry out of their lives. I don't think he loved them. I think he can't love anybody but himself. But I always thought that one day he'd push Kathleen too far and do something so stupid she'd throw him out. And this business of saying he sold his soul is what did it."

"That is what Larry alleged he did."

"Consider the source. Anyone who believes a word Larry says lives to regret it. Like I said before, if this is true, Larry is fooling around with a force way beyond his control. He's like Mickey Mouse in *The Sorcerer's Apprentice*. Only this is something far worse than flooding the basement."

"Very much so."

"Only I'm back at square one. I don't not know if the problems we were having are of natural origin. Larry was too cheap to maintain that house properly. That might explain it. But let's say the problems were supernatural in origin, due to his letting a demon inside."

"Yes."

"Okay. And now the problem was solved with a blessing. Which means, pardon my French, this damn thing, I'm reluctant to speak its name, is banned from getting inside our house. And it can't hurt me. Or my sister. Or the kids, or even our cats."

"Dante and Virgil, yes."

"My question is, if you threw it out of 2 Split Tree Circle, where did it go?"

"Ah. Good question, Grace. Let's see what Our Lord has to tell us about that." Father Flynn reached for his Bible. "Here we go. Matthew, chapter 13, verses 43–45. 'When an unclean spirit goes out of a person it roams through arid regions searching for rest but finds none. Then it says, "I will return to my home from which I came," But upon returning, it finds it empty, swept clean, and put in order. Then it goes and brings back with itself seven other spirits more evil than itself and they move in and dwell there; and the last condition of that person is worse than the first. Thus it will be with this evil generation.'"

"How do you read that, Father? This thing isn't back in Hell? It's still hanging around, only trying to bring its friends from Hell with it?"

"It means the unclean spirit may well be still in our world. That it did not go back to Hell, as you say, but might be plotting to do more harm. As for where it went, we don't know, but it went somewhere."

"Kind of creepy."

"And I, for one, will not tolerate the idea of any harm coming to those children." Father Flynn got out a notepad. "Here is my cell number. If anything out of the ordinary should occur, anything you call creepy, please don't hesitate to contact me at any time of the day or night. I'll notify Cardinal Kelly and take it from there if I must. But the safety of those children has to come first."

"Thanks, Father. That really means a lot. Now, may I ask you another question, which is going to sound a bit silly?"

"Certainly."

"Did you watch *Sing! Sing! Sing!* last Wednesday?"

"No, I've never been into that sort of thing, which is a pity. I understand there was a lady from St. Catherine's on and that she's going up to the next level. So, I just might see how she does."

"Thanks so much for everything, Father," Grace told him. "So will we."

43

Larry had reason to regret starting the rumor that Dorothy was sick with a virus. A lot more flowers were delivered to the front yard.

"What am I going to do with them all?" he lamented. "There's enough out there to sink a battleship!"

Then the messages started pouring in. "'We all hope you are feeling better soon,' from Jared, LaShawn, and Longianna. Plus a lot more, from people we never heard of! When will it ever end?"

Dorothy was able to do some interviews with the media, though Larry knew that would only make things worse. She did an interview on Channel 8. There was an article about her in the *Clarion*. The only result was more flowers and get-well wishes.

Did the McGrath sisters see any of her publicity? Dorothy certainly hoped so. Served them right!

"I wish there were some way to convert all of this to cash," Larry lamented. Dorothy was forced to get her phone number changed and unlisted. Larry was constantly reminded of the dark side: not fans but all those creditors who were not going to get paid anything soon.

The date of the next show drew nearer. "You have to keep practicing," Larry nagged her. "Singing in the shower isn't going to cut it."

She went to the voice coach Larry had arranged. One night, the voice coach gave Larry some troubling news.

"So, I said to Dorothy, 'What song are you going to sing for the next session?' She wants 'Unchained Melody.' You know, the original was done by a male singer. So that would be a challenge right off. But there have been problems."

"Problems, like what?" Larry asked.

"Like, something's off here. I asked her to do 'And I Will Always Love You' over again. I don't know what went wrong. But she sounded totally different from the way she sounded on TV."

"Different, how?"

"Different, terrible! I've never heard a worse rendition. I had to ask her to get closer to the key in which it was written. Are you sure this is the same Dorothy Walsh I saw? Or has she got an untalented identical twin? They look alike but don't sound alike at all. There's no fire in this one, no spirit. I don't see how she managed to do so well."

A furious Larry sacked him, refused to pay his bill, and hired another voice coach. "Don't tell me how she's doing," Larry warned him. "Just get her up to speed. You know she's got what it takes to win, but I'm worried about that fat guy. He could be the spoiler."

Dorothy herself wasn't helping. She was changing her mind about "Unchained Melody." *Maybe I should do something from Broadway*, she was thinking. *Like "Memories," from* Cats.

"Oh, please!" Larry begged her. "You're going to have to start rehearsing soon with the musicians who are backing you up. In Hollywood. And I can't be there with you. And you know damn well why. The least you can do is tell them what you're singing!"

Inside, Dorothy felt relief that Larry was not allowed to come with her. She had all the help she could possibly need. Larry would only be a distraction. "Do this, that, and the other thing my way!" Her guardian angel told her that was the path to losing.

That night, she was in bed between a snoring Larry and Roach. "He never makes love to me anymore," she told Roach.

"I noticed. Do you know why? He's nothing but a self-centered slob."

"Do you think he said he loves me only because I'm supposed to be rich and famous?"

"You know the answer to that. He was so indifferent to the splendor of your voice until you won the first level. Now, he wants to take over. Everything has to be done his way."

"He's getting to be so domineering. Always butting in."

Dorothy closed her eyes and felt the comfort of Roach's presence.

For an instant, she pitied Kathleen, who had spent so many years married to Larry. She even pitied Bobby and Jeanine, forced to grow up with his shouting and griping.

"Nothing is right! Everything you do is wrong!"

"Don't even think about them," Roach crooned to her. "Besides, since you never married him, all you need to do is kick him to the curb. When you are rich and famous."

"You think I will win? Lately, it's been hard. Larry has me working with a coach. But sometimes I can't reach the right notes. I never had that problem before. The more I force myself, the worse I sound. Guardian angel, I can't go on live TV sounding like this."

"But you will," Roach promised her. "All you have to do is relax. And you will be sensational."

44

The countdown to the second level had started. Dorothy's vast number of suitcases were being loaded into an airport van. She had to be in Hollywood tomorrow to begin rehearsals with her backup musicians.

"Will you miss me, darling?" she asked as he offered her a modest peck on the cheek.

"Oh, a lot, honey. So much!"

"You will watch me?"

"Natch! If not here, then on the jumbo screen at the Round Robin. They said they'd have you on. A round of drinks on the house when you win."

"That's so nice of them."

Dorothy got into the van and was on her way to the airport, where she would catch the usual Flight 238. Larry waited until the van was out of sight.

"Now!" he said, rubbing his hands. "Time to get moving!"

He thought of George, a real attorney, for whose advice he was paying so dearly. George forbade him to go to Hollywood with Dorothy.

"But he said nothing about going to Hollywood without Dorothy!"

To think, at first he thought that Dorothy had the chances of a snowball in Hell of winning. He was so sure that her passing the audition was only a fluke. How wrong he had been.

Winning was within her grasp. All she had to do was to reach out and grab that brass ring. Then record a killer CD. That should occur about the time the judge banged his gavel down. "Divorce granted!"

And so what if Kathleen was awarded everything? He and Dorothy would then get married. Then buy a home of their own. Forget Swan Pointe. What a dump compared to Malibu! There, they would lead a happy, child-free life with a staff of servants.

"It's the least I deserve," Larry reasoned, "considering where I'm going when my life is over."

He went back into Dorothy's pantry. There, way in the back, was that metal box he had taken from his rolltop desk. The key was taped to the bottom.

"There's a reason I told those brats to stay out of my den. I didn't want them near this."

Larry opened the box. Inside it held $10,000 in cash, mostly tens and twenties.

"This is my emergency fund. Only for me. Kathleen never found out about it. So, Pit Bull doesn't know either. Heh, heh, heh. And since I've maxed all but one of my credit cards, if ever there were an emergency, this is it."

Larry stuffed bills into his wallet and his money belt. Then he packed his bags and called Uber to take him to the airport.

"Dorothy owes me everything," he reasoned. "She could never have gotten so far without me. And if something starts to go wrong, I will have to be with her. And I can't do that from the Round Robin."

At the airport, he went to the ticket desk. "Excuse me, miss," he said. "Might I buy a ticket for Flight 238 to LAX?"

"I'm sorry, sir," the attendant replied. "Flight 238 has already departed."

"Dammit to hell!" said Larry, thinking, *Perfect.* "When is the next departure for Los Angeles?"

"That will be Flight 369, leaving in another two hours."

"One coach ticket for 369, please."

"Round-trip?"

"No, um, one-way."

"Will this be on your credit card?"

"Um, yeah."

He showed her his credit card and ID. Larry used the only card not yet maxed out. He thought of paying in twenties. If he did that, he might as well wear a tag that said, *Hello! My name is ISIS!* Very important, he thought, not to call any attention to himself. The TSA check was quick and painless.

Once up in the air, Larry tried to plan out his next step. Getting a hotel room ought to be easy. Dorothy was at the Marriott, so he'd have to find someplace else. But how was he going to get into the studio? No doubt, Dorothy's show was already sold out. And security was going to be tight.

Then it occurred to him: it was going to be NFL night.

"Easy as pie! I'll just sneak in as one of the Ravens."

Larry could not see anything out of the window; he was beside the wing. He let his mind drift back to when he was the star quarterback at Jesuit High. He had told amazing tales of his gridiron glory. Many believed him.

Only not a word was true. He did try out for the team. He never forgot his humiliation when the coach stopped the tryout with "Before Kavanaugh gets himself killed!"

The coach left him with a final bitter message. "Remember, Kavanaugh, there is no *I* in *team*."

The closest he came to being a player was a seat in the stands. He memorized what the real quarterback did and claimed credit for it in years to come. If people wanted to believe him, it was their own business.

Although Kathleen believed him at first, her mother never did. And Grace? She laughed at him. She actually laughed.

"Whatever," Larry reminded himself. "I'll be rid of that crazy family soon enough. They will be watching me on *At Home with the Stars* while they're still stuck in a split-level on Split Tree. Too bad!"

"Ladies and Gentlemen, we are about to begin our descent into Los Angeles International Airport. Kindly return to your seats, fasten your seat belts, and leave your trays in the upright position. It's eighty-six degrees on the ground and clear."

"California dreaming is becoming a reality," Larry hummed to himself.

The terminal was far more chaotic and crowded that he expected. It took him a while to find the right luggage carousel. As he picked up his bags, he saw two young men across the way. He felt he should know them but could not quite place them. One was white, the other was a Hindu-looking fellow in a turban. He wore a T-shirt that said Computer Repair. They were laughing their heads off. Larry wondered what they found so amusing.

Whatever, it was too unlikely he'd find anyone he knew in a madhouse like this.

45

The day arrived. Dorothy, in her suite at the Marriott, lay on her bed as Roach instructed.

"Remember," Scorch cautioned Roach. "Once this is done, you can't shape-shift any more. You will appear to be Dorothy Walsh, unless you make your true form visible. You can't pass yourself off as Johnny LaRoche or anyone else. Are you sure you know what you're doing?"

"Please! I've already broken her free will, made her to do the worst thing she can imagine."

"Remember—if you get caught by an exorcist, you will be on your own. Old Scratch won't let any of us assist you."

"That jerk always did underestimate me. He will see how wrong he was."

"Let me tell you something. You really need to know this. Right now, we're in the archdiocese of Los Angeles."

"So what? Big deal."

"I'm not even allowed to say this. But you know, I'm often alone in Old Scratch's office when he's not in. And I have all his passwords. And I've seen his top-secret files. He has a file on every exorcist in this world. But as for the senior one in Los Angeles, I swear, that file must be a mile thick. He's that good, Roach. One of the all-time best. A real holy terror. And this is your first possession, after all."

"So much the better when I chew him up and spit him out."

"Roach, do you have any idea what it's like to be Tased? Because that's what he's going to do to you."

"I've taken Dorothy this far. This will be my masterpiece. I'm not going to turn back now."

"Okay. Go for it. Lots of luck."

"Now, close your eyes, darling," Roach whispered. "That's good. Now take a deep breath and let it out slowly. Another. Now, this time, Dorothy, you are going to breathe me deep inside of you. Are you ready?"

"Yes. I will obey you."

"And only me?"

"Forever, my love. Take me as your own."

"One, two, three, breathe."

Dorothy started slowly, then ended with a sharp gasp.

"Remember how good it felt to have Larry inside of you? Isn't this better?"

"Ay! Infinitely so!"

Roach let himself spread through every cell of Dorothy's body. His talons sunk all the way into her corrupted spirit. Even her fingers and toes were of Roach. Roach looked around through Dorothy's eyes. He even felt a certain pang where baby Moira used to be. Through the window, he saw planes landing at LAX. He could hear the air conditioner and feel its chill on his bare skin. He got up and looked at himself in the mirror.

"You did it!" Scorch gaped at his battle buddy, now in the form of a woman. "Roach! What's it like?"

"Beyond my wildest imaginings," Roach replied in Dorothy's voice. Roach was so high on it he felt as if he had the real Dante and Virgil there, writing down his every word.

"Roach, let's hear you!"

From Dorothy's throat came a threatening masculine growl: "Sic transit gloria mundi!"

"Wow! Can you spin her head around? Let's see!"

"I most certainly can," Roach said, "but not now. She has to be in perfect shape because she's putting on a show tonight. I can't afford to have her damaged. Not yet. For now, Dorothy and I are going to take a shower together. Then we're going to put on that gown. Meanwhile, you go back to Hell and tell our jerk of a boss to watch *Sing! Sing! Sing!* tonight. He will never dump on me again."

46

Zero minus one hour and counting.

Larry discovered where the Baltimore Ravens were staying and waited for them in the lobby. All he had to do was mix in with them. Nothing could be easier. Then a whole flock of Ravens emerged from the elevator.

All Larry could think was, *D'oh!*

It was one thing to watch them play on a TV screen. Quite another to see them up close and in person. Every one of them looked like a human/Mack truck hybrid. Larry knew there was no way he could be mistaken for one of them. There was one thought more terrifying than facing Pit Bull in divorce court. That was having one of these moving mountains charging right at him in an arena.

The lobby was already full of their fans chanting, "Nevermore!"

Larry snuck out through the revolving door. "What was I thinking?" he asked himself. "Time for plan B. What is plan B?"

He was near the studio where *Sing! Sing! Sing!* was about to begin. There were several people in line, holding tickets. He looked at them with envy. If only there were a way to get his hands on one. What to do?

"Pssst. Pal," someone whispered to him from an alley. "You wanna get in to see the show?"

"It's sold out. Has been for the past month."

"You want a ticket?"

"Well, yeah, but ..."

The scalper held out a ticket. "You want it? Twenty-five hundred dollars. Terms: cash."

"This had better not be a fake!"

"Take a look." The scalper grasped it tightly. It did look exactly like the real ones.

"Now, this seat's kind of in the back."

"So much the better," Larry said. "I don't want to be on camera."

"This is kind of behind the camera."

Thus, George and Pit Bull, were they watching, could not see Larry. Neither would Dorothy know he was there. Someone once told Larry that a performer on stage could not see beyond the first row.

"Make up your mind quick. This is a limited time offer, pal."

"Two grand?"

"Twenty-five hundred, final offer."

"All right! You got a deal!"

It took a while for Larry to count out that much in tens and twenties. "Enjoy the show," the scalper said and vanished down the alley.

The ticket turned out to be valid. An usher showed Larry to his seat, way in the rear. His view of the stage was pretty poor. In the distance, he could see technicians running around and Longianna Rae and LaShawn Curry talking and laughing.

Could it be they were laughing at him, like he thought those two dudes in the airport were?

As a vantage point, this seat was terrible. But it gave him a measure of control. If something went wrong, he'd be ready.

Zero minus two minutes and counting. Suddenly, Father Flynn remembered that one of the ladies from St. Catherine's was going to be on *Sing! Sing! Sing!* tonight. He had almost forgotten. He turned the TV on. A parade of inane commercials was in progress.

Then the volume went up with "Welcome, America! Welcome to level two of *Sing! Sing! Sing!* And have we got some great songs for you tonight!"

The emcee went on to praise the NFL and its various charities and to introduce the Baltimore Ravens. "Stand up and take a bow!"

Father Flynn found the loud volume and the flashing lights distracting. The emcee went on to introduce Jared Winters, LaShawn Curry, and Longianna Rae. Then he brought out the contestants. Dorothy Walsh was going to be near the end.

Perhaps she's so good no one wants to follow her, Father Flynn was thinking. But for now, he'd turn the TV off and recite his evening prayers. That sort of program could give one a headache. At this time of day, he needed peace and quiet.

Suddenly the phone on his desk sprang to life. The number that popped up was that of Kavanaugh, Lawrence P.

"Hello?" he said. "Speaking. Yes, who is this, please?"

It was a woman's voice, and she sounded deeply troubled.

"Kathleen Kavanaugh? Of course I remember you and those amazing children. Am I what? Watching *Sing! Sing! Sing!* I was a moment ago. Now I see the lady from St. Catherine's won't be on any time soon, so … Excuse me? Dante and Virgil? Oh, you mean the cats, yes, your sister's cats! Ms. Kavanaugh, could you slow down a bit? I'm having some trouble following what you are trying to tell me. That's better."

The voice coming through the phone explained, "You said to call if anything creepy took place. I'm afraid it just did."

"All right. Take a deep breath, and tell me what happened."

"Those cats. They are very friendly cats. And they never have shown any reaction to what's on TV. But just now, when the camera was on Dorothy … I've never seen anything like it! They jumped up and snarled and spat at the screen. Their fur stood on end. Then they panicked and ran up to Jeanine's room. They're under Jeanine's bed, meowing. Like they're trying to tell us something."

"Ms. Kavanaugh, is Grace there?"

"No, she's trying to reach them under the bed. But she can't reach far enough."

"This does sound unusual. And I must admit I'm no authority on feline behavior. Something spooked them. I'd advise Grace not to try to force them out or risk getting scratched. No, we can't have that. Just have Grace and the children present for them till they quiet down. They will be calmed by having the persons around who love them. Please have Grace call me once she's free. In the meantime, keep watching the program, and I will too. Let me know if anything else unforeseen takes place."

"I will, Father. I just don't want anything bad to happen."

"No one does, Ms. Kavanaugh. I'm right here if you need me."

Father Flynn hung up. "No, we don't want anything bad to happen. Especially in front of an audience that could number in the millions."

He turned on the TV with the volume down low, so he'd know when this Dorothy came on, then opened up his prayer book. He could hardly believe how obese the next contestant was. The emcee introduced him as Tony from Jersey City.

"Tony, you blew us away at level one with your rendition of Sinatra. Something tells me the chairman of the board was looking down and smiling on you. What are you going to sing for us this time?"

"Something different. My mom's watching. Hi, Mom! I want to dedicate this to her. It's her favorite: 'Ave Maria.'"

"Take it away, Tony!"

Father Flynn had to admit Tony's vocal range was fantastic. Still, Grace's question came back to him. "Where did it go?"

"When an unclean spirit goes out of a person, it roams through regions searching for rest and finds none."

It went someplace. Where?

He had heard talk from St. Catherine's; the other ladies were concerned about Dorothy. She had been acting strangely. Not like herself at all. There was gossip that she was involved with a married man. Who knew if there was any truth to it? Could it be that someone was envious of her success?

As Edgar Allen Poe might say: only this and nothing more.

47

Roach heard a tiny voice inside him, as if someone were trapped in the bottom of a deep well.

"Someone help me, please! Let me out!"

"Shut up, Dorothy. Not one more peep out of you till I say to start singing!"

Dorothy/Roach was still backstage with the others who had not gone on yet. She could hear and see everything on the monitor. First, the emcee was telling big Tony that Frank Sinatra was looking down on him from heaven, smiling.

That was an outrage. But "Ave Maria" was like waving a red cape in front of a bull. It was the next worst thing to having that fatso recite aloud from *The Divine Comedy*. Showing off all the cantos where Roach should have been! And was not! He wanted to kill them all, starting now.

"Dorothy?" another contestant asked. "You feel all right?"

"I'm just a bit nervous," Roach replied in Dorothy's voice. "Excuse me. I'm going to the ladies' room."

"Sure. Let us know if you need anything."

Dorothy/Roach went into the posh ladies' room and locked the door. Dorothy's face in the mirror was bright red.

"Let us know if you need anything! Hypocrites! They'd rather see me dead than in their way!"

Dorothy/Roach trembled with white-hot rage, then assumed the form of an angry demon.

He then ripped the sink out of the wall and smashed it against the stall. Then he pulled the stall door off and yanked the toilet off the floor.

A deluge soaked the rest of the lounge. He pulled the mirror down and shattered it, then destroyed the vanity and chairs.

Dorothy/Roach paused to admire his handwork. "As Karen Carpenter once said, we've only just begun." Then he changed again into the form of Dorothy and returned to the waiting area.

"Feel better now?"

"Much better," the Dorothy voice said. "I was just a tad overheated."

"Best thing is a drink of water."

"Truer words were never spoken."

At that point, a janitor noticed a torrent pouring under the ladies' room door and called the engineer. "We got a problem! A water problem!"

Far away, a phone rang again. "Father Flynn? This is Grace."

"Yes, Grace, has anything else untoward taken place in your home? The children are safe? What about the cats?"

"The cats are still under Jeanine's bed. They won't come out, but they're acting calmer. The children are staying with them. That seems to help."

"So, no other disturbances?"

"None so far. You know this person I was telling you about? Dorothy Walsh? She's on next. I think they're about to introduce her."

"Yes, I see. Here she is now."

"And what are you going to sing for us tonight, Dorothy?" the emcee asked.

"Hey!" Grace shouted. "Father, did you see that?"

Dorothy's eyes rolled all the way so only the whites showed, and she collapsed in a heap at the emcee's feet.

Chaos broke forth in the studio. A technician gave a signal, "Cut to commercial."

Longianna Rae and LaShawn Curry pleaded for quiet. "Remember," LaShawn announced, "this happened to Marie Osmond on *Dancing with the Stars*. It is no big deal."

Jared Winters looked lost. The emcee asked if there was a doctor in the house. Apparently, not. LaShawn Curry and Longianna Rae went over to Dorothy.

There was another disturbance in the rear seats. Security was summoned. A man who was claiming to be either Dorothy's boyfriend or manager tried to get up on the stage, but the guards held him back. "Darling!" he shouted. "It's me! Larry! Please let me go to her!"

Larry was still not allowed on stage. To anyone who would listen, he repeated, "She's been sick, caught a virus, been working so hard, just wore herself out!"

Amid the uproar, the building engineer appeared, shouting about a catastrophe involving plumbing fixtures.

Dorothy opened her eyes. Longianna Rae helped her up. In spite of the red coloring in Dorothy's face, her skin felt freezing cold.

"Can you stand up?" the emcee asked.

"Dorothy! Dorothy!" Larry shouted.

"Security, throw that bum out of here. Okay, she's all right. Aren't you, Dorothy? You feel up to singing for us? Good! Back in your seats, everyone. Okay, let's go live!"

"So call, click, or visit your local Toyota dealer today!" was followed by an immediate return to the program in progress. Dorothy stood in the middle of the stage, held up by Longianna Rae, with the emcee demanding a big hand "for the little lady who is about to sing her heart out for us. Dorothy, take it away!"

Dorothy did not sing. Instead, a deep growl came out of her.

"I am not Dorothy," it thundered. "The next person who calls me Dorothy dies! Don't you know that my name is Roach and I have long talons and strong fists?"

So saying, Roach rammed Dorothy's tiny fist into Longianna Rae with the force of a wrecking ball, knocking her out cold. He then picked up and heaved the emcee into the audience as screams rang forth. He threw a punch at Jared Winters, breaking his jaw, then tackled LaShawn Curry and wrapped his hands around LaShawn's throat.

At that point, the Baltimore Ravens stormed the stage and landed on top of Roach. There were at least ten of them trying to break the grip of Roach's hands.

"This ain't real!" the powerful halfback said.

"I am real, and you are not!" Roach replied. Thinking he had applied enough pressure to kill LaShawn, he let her go. When he stood up, he threw the entire offensive line of the Ravens off of him. Then he ran, plowing down all who stood in his way. He ran out the exit, into the alley, and vanished.

Police and first responders took over the stage, all demanding to know, "Where did that thing go?" The live feed was cut off. A long infomercial followed.

"My God, my God!" Grace wept. "Father, did you see that? Now, we know where it went!"

"*Non praevalebunt*, Grace. That means the gates of Hell shall not prevail."

Dorothy/Roach kept running, till the crowds around the studio thinned out, till Roach's hearing picked up a familiar voice close by.

"You have to let me back in there!" a man was shouting. "You have no idea of what it cost me to get in. Who am I? I'm her fiancé, that's who!"

As passersby screamed, Dorothy/Roach picked up Larry as if he were nothing more than a sack of dirty laundry, threw Larry over his shoulder, and took off like a cheetah in the direction of the Hollywood Hills.

48

In a distant kitchen, Kathleen asked her sister and Father Flynn if they wanted coffee.

"That would help," Grace agreed.

"Even if it is an unholy hour of the night," Father Flynn agreed. "And again, I apologize for having to come to you at a time like this. But perhaps you might have some information about this ... this ..."

"Thing," said Grace. "If it is really the same thing that Larry let in here."

"Yes. Also, I've been in contact with my colleagues in Los Angeles. Several of them are experienced exorcists, and they have spoken with Ms. Rae, who is now awake and alert."

"Thank God," the sisters agreed.

"All of the injured were taken to Cedars-Sinai."

"Did that thing kill anyone?"

"Not that we know of, and not for lack of trying. Ms. Curry had the most severe injuries. Her condition is listed as serious but stable."

Grace observed that the real heroes were the Baltimore Ravens, even though several of them would be sidelined.

"And what about Jared Winters? Jeanine was upset about him."

"He sustained non-life-threatening injuries."

"I'll tell her in the morning. She's going to send him a get-well card."

"That is most kind of Jeanine. Did the children actually see what took place?

"Do you mean when, again, pardon my French, but all hell broke loose on *Sing! Sing! Sing!*" Grace asked.

"That is a most apt term," Father Flynn told her.

"They did not. They were upstairs, with the cats."

"Speaking of which," said Grace.

"Meow? Meow?"

"Come on in, guys. No, you can't have coffee. Why? You are cats, and cats don't like it. Have some tuna instead."

"Dante and Virgil?" Father Flynn asked. "We've met. Beautiful cats." They gave Father Flynn a gracious greeting.

"This is the way they act all the time. Virgil's the one in the white toga. Dante's the noble Florentine. Now, you said you wanted some information from us."

"About this possessed person. The name I have is Dorothy Marie Walsh. Now, I don't know her that well. It seems she's a member of St. Catherine's."

"You don't know her that well?" Grace asked. "Lucky you."

"I'm afraid, Father, that Dorothy and ourselves go way back," Kathleen said. "Back to when Dorothy and I were in second grade." Kathleen recounted Dorothy's cruelty to both of them and how it resulted in her being expelled.

"Eighty-sixed from second grade, can you believe?" Grace asked.

"I recently made a decision," Kathleen said, "to tell the children the truth about the incident. As always, Bobby nailed it with the perfect word. He called her a bully."

"Has Dorothy done anything to either one of you since then?"

"Yes," said Kathleen. "If Dorothy were Captain Ahab, we were her white whale. She blamed us for her expulsion, which, in her mind, cancelled a concert. She was supposed to be the soloist. All our fault!"

Father Flynn wrote something down. "So, she never thought that it was in any way her own fault?"

"Nope!" said Grace. "Nothing was ever Dorothy's fault."

"After we were grown, and I'd married Larry, she did attempt contact with me. A let-bygones-be-bygones sort of thing. Of course, I didn't trust her. I knew she was up to something. And that something was a threat of blackmailing me. Oh, she never actually tried to get money. But she made a clear threat, and I reacted badly. I was terrified by it."

Father Flynn kept writing notes.

"And about Larry," Kathleen went on. "My husband, soon to be my ex. It's come to my attention that he's been having an affair with Dorothy."

"Oh my dear Lord," was Father Flynn's response.

"Is Larry still AWOL?" Grace asked.

"Yes. That's something else," said Kathleen. "He's taken leave of his job."

"He's taken leave of his senses," Grace said.

"It seems a few days ago, his boss tried to get hold of him. He has a project long overdue. He won't answer his cell. He was known to be living in Dorothy's house. So, his boss called the cops and had them do a wellness check over there. Like Grace did for that poor man who died up the street."

"Floyd Ferguson," said Grace. "He had been dead for several days in that house."

"That boarded-up house?" asked Father Flynn.

"That's the one. Anyhow, they could not find a trace of Larry at all. Dead or alive. He hasn't even called his own divorce lawyer. Now he's listed as a missing person. The cops are trying to find out his whereabouts through recent credit card transactions. They said they'd let me know if any turn up."

"This is just a normal day for Larry." Grace sighed. "Mr. Irresponsible, all the way."

Father Flynn put his notepad away. "I need to thank you both for the information you have given. I'll pass it on to the archdiocese of Los Angeles. Have either one of you had any experience with exorcism before?"

"Just in thriller books and up on the silver screen."

"Then let me give you some idea of what is really going to take place. It appears that this Dorothy is in a fully possessed stage. Which is rare. From what I have been able to learn about her, she has not been acting like herself of late. That could be a sign of a demonic attack as a lead-up to a possession.

"You must understand, a demon cannot walk in on you. He must be invited into your home, your physical body, whatever. He can use flattery and deception to get in. But the victim has to give him consent to enter."

The land line phone in the living room rang. "I'll get it," said Kathleen. "Hello? Yes? This is Kathleen Kavanaugh. No, there's been no contact for me or either of his children. No call, no email, zero, ziltch, nada. What have you got? I see! Thanks so much, and please call at any time if something else turns up."

Kathleen returned to the kitchen. "The cops," she said. "They found that Larry used his credit card for a one-way flight to LA a few days ago. Then he took a hotel room. Then the credit card company cut him off, so no more charges."

"Hi-yo, Silver!" said Grace. "The credit card kid rides again!"

"I'm sorry, Father. Did I miss something?"

"I was explaining to Grace how demons work. They don't have the power to do anything to you without the consent of your free will. They want to break your free will. How do they do this? This brings us back to the seven deadly sins. That's what the demon works with. He looks for your weak points.

"Now, from what little I know of Dorothy Walsh, she was, at one time, in charge of the pro-life committee at St. Catherine's. She was often seen in front of the abortion facility on Twelfth Street. Holding up a life-sized plastic fetus."

"Sheeesh," said Grace.

"I was bothered by what Kathleen told me. Because I had been willing to believe in Dorothy's veneer, that she was an exemplary Catholic, even a consecrated virgin. For such a person to have an affair with a married man did not seem possible. But now, it makes perfect sense. If this demon had been working with her for a while, he would gradually have her doing things she would ordinarily find offensive. There will reach a point where her free will is shattered. Then she is at the mercy of the demon, who can possess her whenever he wants."

"We've heard other things," said Grace. "Financial irregularities. Even auditioning for *Sing! Sing! Sing!* We knew she had a pretty good voice. She was so proud of it."

"One of the seven deadlies," Father Flynn told her. "The worst of the bunch as it opens up a path to six others. And there is one other thing you must be aware of. Does that laptop have the tape of the incident?"

"Of course!" said Kathleen. "Here!"

"Ooops," said Grace, "I'd better put Dante and Virgil in the sunroom. Come on, guys."

"Now back it up to where it says to visit your local Toyota dealer today. Good. Hit play. Now there is Dorothy, with the emcee on her right, and Longianna Rae on her left, helping her up."

"Let's have a big hand for the little lady who is about to sing her heart out for us!" the emcee shouted over the applause. "Dorothy, take it away!"

"Watch closely here."

A loud growl came out of Dorothy's throat. *"I am not!"* Someone screamed. Dorothy's fist slammed into Longianna Rae. "Stop there," said Father Flynn.

"Ow!" the sisters both said. "That must really hurt."

"Did you hear what the demon said?"

"I am not! Then there was too much noise."

"Run it again. No, we can't make out anything beyond *I am not.*"

"That's why our technicians have been working so hard on this recording. To hear the name. Thus far, without success."

Kathleen thought. "If God's real name is I Am, doesn't it add up that the demon's name is I Am Not?"

"Possibly. But about the way demons work: they don't want you to know their real names. To name something gives you power over it. That's the last thing they want. Kathleen, did Larry ever tell you the name of the demon he had in here?"

"I'm trying to remember!"

"Larry forgot it too. That's why he told us the demon's name was Mr. Stink Bug."

"Only it wasn't Stink Bug. LaRoche! That was it! Johnny LaRoche!"

"I can assure you his name is not Johnny LaRoche. Or Stink Bug. A demon will always lie to you about his name. He will never reveal it unless he's under a lot of stress and slips up. Which is why a ritual exorcism always starts with demanding the demon's name. And expecting lies for the first attempts. One has to get that demon under extreme pressure before he will tell you his true name. And that is why we're so fortunate that Longianna Rae was able to speak with the exorcist in Los Angeles. We have cause to believe that he did reveal his name to her."

Father Flynn turned his notes back to the beginning and read: "Here is what he said: 'I am not Dorothy. The next person who calls me Dorothy dies! Don't you know that my name is Roach and I have long talons and strong fists?'" And then he sent a thought to Ms. Rae. *I have been in your world for many months. I have killed. And know this, Longianna Rae, you are next.*

Grace made the sign of the cross. "I'm scared," Kathleen admitted. "That thing was in here. In that den."

"It's not coming back, Kathleen," Father Flynn assured her. "It cannot hurt you."

The silence that followed was shattered by the tone of bells. "That my cell?" Grace asked.

"No, it's mine," Father Flynn replied. The incoming number lit up with a 213 area code. "Yes? Speaking. Yes. I see. We can get something on a closed circuit. Let me know what you think is best. I'll go to the cardinal's office right now."

Father Flynn ended the call. "If you will excuse me, I need to get downtown quickly. It seems that a citizen called in a complaint to the LAPD about a woman, presumed to be high on drugs, kidnapping a man right off of a sidewalk. Do you know about the Hollywood sign, up on a hill?"

"Yes!" they replied.

"This woman is now seated in the delta of the letter Y. She's holding the man in her lap and singing about 'The Good Ship Lollipop.' It is dedicated to both of you."

49

The first step was to impose a news blackout around the Hollywood sign. Then traffic was diverted away. Only police and fire vehicles were allowed beyond the barrier. A safety net was put up around the base of the letter Y.

A chopper had been sent in, lowered over the Y, and a ladder dropped. Roach grabbed the ladder and pulled. The other end of the ladder had to be dropped from the chopper, or Roach could have pulled the whole thing down, killing everyone aboard. Then, a no-fly zone was established.

Roach's voice boomed out of Dorothy. "What a pity that would have been! How many of those brave rescuers might I have killed?"

Darkness fell on the Hollywood Hills along with a brutal downpour. A spotlight focused on the letter Y.

"We don't know how much power this thing has, what it can do," the commander on the ground told his crew. "Now, if this were some little thing, like King Kong on top of the Empire State Building, we might have a pretty good idea of what its limitations are. But we have no idea."

"And this is supposed to be a demonic possession?" one of his crew asked.

"Yes, and the archdiocese is supposed to be sending their best exorcist now. Let's hope he gets here before this situation gets any worse. That woman is Dorothy Walsh, and she is the one possessed. Yes, *the* Dorothy Walsh. The guy in her lap is supposed to be her fiancé. Or manager. Or something. Remember we want to get rid of this thing without hurting either one of them. Yes? Question?"

"How did, um, she and her boyfriend get up that high?"

"We have reason to believe they flew. Or, she flew and carried him."

There were sounds of incredulity.

"I've been told that the ability to levitate is a symptom of demonic possession. Along with supernatural physical strength. Which Dorothy has shown us. Just ask the Ravens. Now, if there are no more questions, can we all get in our places?"

Someone muttered, "I wish I were back in Iraq."

Roach, who had been silent, suddenly spoke up.

"Did you enjoy that, Kathleen and Grace McGrath? I certainly hope so, and there is so much more where it came from. And for my next number ..."

"Somebody please help me!" the man cried out.

"Shut up! I am not going to warn you again! I am the ventriloquist. You are my wooden dummy. Don't you forget it."

It then addressed the first responders on the ground. "Larry here is my lover. You know that? Yes, he is, my little snookie-poo! Know that Lawrence Paul Kavanaugh Junior here, so-called attorney at law, but we know better, don't we, honey-bunch, is under contract to me! Sold himself to me! Signed, sealed, and delivered himself to me! He did it cheap too. I get body, mind, and, above all, his soul. Mine! All mine! And you know something else? Larry and I are getting married. Tonight!"

To Larry, Roach said: "Keep your mouth shut till I tell you to say, 'I do.' Yes, I saw inside your rotten mind. You didn't give a damn about Dorothy's career till she was about to make it big. Then you got interested. Real interested in marrying her, moving to Malibu, leeching off Dorothy for the rest of your miserable life. Know that I hereby accept your gracious proposal of marriage. Only you ain't gonna end up in no Malibu."

A police van approached, and a black-clad man got out. "I'm the senior exorcist from the archdiocese of Los Angeles." He looked up at the delta of the Y and recoiled in disgust.

"You think this is an actual demonic possession?" the commander asked.

"No question. Absolutely it is."

He was just back from Rome, where he saw Michelangelo's *Pieta* up close. This raving woman, holding the man in her lap, was a blasphemous recreation of Michelangelo's masterpiece. Only a real demon would have the nerve to do anything that vile.

"However, I've got our first step here. That is always to get the demon's real name. I've got it from a reliable source."

"And what is this demon's name?"

"The name I was given is Roach."

"Roach? You mean like a bug?"

"Yes. I must say I have never encountered a demon named Roach before. We have no history together. So, I can't predict what it will do next."

"Look at it this way, Father. He never met you. So, he doesn't know what to expect either. Do you think Roach has pulled this crap off before?"

"We have no way of knowing, and we don't want to know either. After you establish the demon's name, there can be no more dialogue. I have only one thing to say to it. You. Out. Now!"

"Sorry, Father, we really can't get you any closer. Did you know that's Dorothy Walsh, the singer? We're not sure what the man's name is. Roach says his name is Lawrence Paul Kavanaugh Junior, which I doubt."

"You did the right thing. Everything a demon says is presumed to be a lie."

"Yeah, but we don't want to damage Dorothy or whoever-he-is any more." Do you think you can do something from down here?"

"Is that netting good and tight, in case they fall?"

"It will catch them, yes."

"I don't expect any success on the first try, but this ought to shake it up a bit."

"Honey, look who's here!" Roach boomed. Then he turned his voice to a high-pitched scream. "Ooohhhh, I'm so scared!"

"Please, Father! Help me!" Larry cried, reaching out.

"Padre, do you do weddings? If so, I take you, Lawrence Paul, as my lawfully wedded prison bitch, to rape and abuse, from this day forward."

"Roach!" the exorcist shouted and then continued in Latin. "Creature of filth, depart now from this servant of God, Dorothy Marie Walsh, and return to the evil pit from whence you came!"

Roach did not realize what would happen next. A wave of pain and nausea swept over him. This was being Tased? It hurt! He felt Dorothy taking advantage of it, trying to wiggle out of his grip. He pulled her in even tighter.

"You try that again, you are going to learn what it means to suffer," Roach warned her. "There is no hope for you, in this world or the next, baby killer."

To Larry, he shouted, "Darling, did you hear what he called me? How dare he!"

Then Roach replied to the exorcist in a blast of obscenities, in flawless Latin.

"How did you learn my name?" Roach thundered. "Who told you?"

The exorcist and the commander got back into the van to confer. "Were you able to shake it?"

"Yes, but it's going to be a hard one to extract. I'd like to call two of my colleagues for backup."

"Anything to squash that Roach."

Larry, already soaking wet, felt a blast of cold air from the second letter L. "Look who's come to see us," Roach told Larry. "My battle buddy from Hell. He's going to be best demon at our wedding. Isn't that right?"

"What wedding?" Scorch said.

"Mine and Larry's, of course, tonight."

"I didn't even know you were in love with that sap, much less getting married."

"Well, we are. And I want all my fellow demons invited."

"Um, sure. But look. There's a closed-circuit connection between the archdiocese here and Cardinal Kelly's office. I've hacked it, and it's on the jumbo screen in the Judas Iscariot aula."

"Good work."

"Now, the boss is watching us live."

"Oh, I am simply so impressed. What does he want me to do, wave to the camera?"

"This is serious! He saw you cold-cock Longianna Rae. And for that, he says, if you can bring Dorothy and Larry back to Hell with you, he's going to issue you a pardon."

"Aw, sure he is!"

"He said so. And anything else you want. He's going to have Roach Day in Hell. He'll give you a medal, a triumphal procession through all nine circles, whatever you want."

"Did you ever notice that when he promises you something, what you get is the opposite?"

"He means it, Roach!"

"If he is, tell him here are my demands. The first thing Lord of the Flies is going to do is turn back time, seven hundred years."

"Yeah, but, Roach? That will create a whole new time line."

"So what?"

"So, nobody will be able to get back to here and now. As we know it. There might not even be a here and now."

"Again, so what? This is more important. First *el jerko* turns back time. Then I'm going to talk to Dante and Virgil. And I don't mean those damn cats either. The real ones! They are going to do a complete rewrite of *The Divine Comedy*. The way it should have been written! All about me. And this new and improved *Divine Comedy* is going to be published and will sell as many copies as the old one. If not more! Then I'll be where I should have been all along. The biggest thing in classical literature. This time, it's going to happen, Scorch. This time, it's for real!"

"I'll see what I can do," Scorch said.

"Wasn't he so obsequious and toadying to the real Dante and Virgil! Welcome to Hell, enjoy your stay! It was sickening. Oh, don't forget to invite everybody to the wedding."

"Have there been any attempts to exorcise you?" Scorch asked.

"So far, one, and it was pathetic." Roach would not admit to how badly it burned.

"Was it that holy terror I told you about?"

"He's no terror if that's the best he can do."

"Watch out, bro! That's one of his tricks. He'll give you a few light taps at first. Just to loosen your grip. Then, when you least expect it, bang! Zoom!"

"He had my real name. I'm going to kill whoever told him."

"We'd better think about that later. I'd better get back and give Old Scratch your message."

"You do that. Remember. Wedding tonight."

"Sure."

Roach looked around. That spotlight was bothering him. That rain kept up, harder than ever. Two more police vans appeared. Larry whimpered.

"Oh, look at you. What a disgrace." Larry's clothing was soaking. "Surely you have no intention of wearing that mess to your wedding? You'd be better off with nothing at all."

So saying, Roach pulled off Larry's clothing, bit by bit, and dropped it into the net below. Keys to Dorothy's house. Cell phone. Shoes. Wallet. Inside the wallet, the commander found a driver's license issued to Lawrence Paul Kavanaugh Junior. There was a money belt with several thousand dollars in soggy bills. Plop, splash.

"You look like Adam in Eden. Naked and afraid. You should be. Much improved."

By now, it was midnight. Two more exorcists got out of the other vans. Roach could hear them planning with their senior member.

"On the count of three," they agreed, "we hit that thing. And we hit it hard."

"Are you here for this evening's entertainment?" Roach roared at them. "You are just in time!" Roach proceeded to commit indecent acts upon Larry.

The ploy did not work. It only seemed to infuriate them.

"Hold on, babe. It's going to be a bumpy evening." Roach steeled himself.

"*Unus! Duo! Tres! Roach!*"

Roach shrieked in pain and kept holding on. This time, the level of agony was almost unbearable.

50

The light was still on in the Kavanaugh kitchen. "What time is it?" Kathleen asked.

"Just about 3:00 a.m." Grace kept her eyes fixed on an image of the Hollywood sign on the laptop.

"So, just about midnight in LA."

"Yeah."

"And nothing yet?"

"Father Flynn said he'd call the minute there was any change." The phone was still.

Grace stood up, stretched, and looked into the sunroom. Dante and Virgil were curled up together on the glider. As long as they did not see what was on the laptop, they were fine.

"I keep thinking, that guy with Dorothy, who else could it be?" Kathleen wondered.

"Of course, it's Larry. Where there's trouble, there's Larry. He never did have to look for trouble; it finds him."

"I wonder if he's still alive."

"I just don't know, sis."

"It would be nice if we could see what's going on."

"But we can't because of the news blackout."

"Imagine what would happen if this were live on CNN?"

"You wouldn't want to see it."

Grace placed her finger on the letter Y. Kathleen wondered again how Larry and Dorothy got there.

"The same way Dumbo got into the tree is how. Remember—that's not Dorothy; that's Roach."

"You said once you didn't want to even mention his name."

"I'm not scared of that damn thing anymore. I'll say whatever I want. Roach, Roach, Roach! Screw you, Roach. Did you know that roaches can fly?"

"That one sure did."

The phone rang, and Kathleen jumped on it.

"That was Father Flynn. Three exorcists hit on Roach at once. Three of LA's finest."

"And?"

"And, screaming and yelling. Revolting effluvia. But Roach is holding on. Oh, and it's still raining."

"Damn!"

Grace studied the Y again. "You know something? There was a man long ago. A saint, they said. He lived on top of a pillar."

"What did he do that for?"

"God knows!"

"And here's a demon, doing the same thing. Almost."

"Kind of ridiculous."

"Grace? Do you know how long these things are supposed to take?"

"What? Exorcisms?"

"Yeah."

"We don't know, sis. Some of them can go on for days. Weeks."

"Larry can't survive much longer. If's he's still alive. And neither can Dorothy, even with that Roach inside of her. I never thought I'd say this, but ..."

"But what?"

"I would not wish this off on my worst enemy."

"Neither would I," Grace agreed.

Grace closed the Hollywood sign image and opened up the tape of Sing! Sing! Sing! in slow motion. She took it from the top again. It took long, agonizing minutes for Roach's fist to collide with Longianna Rae.

"You keep looking at that," said Kathleen. "Why? What is it you are looking for?"

"The key is what. This whole thing is locked up, but there has to be a key somewhere. Something we have not even thought of yet. Oh, it's there, sis."

"And you think you can find it?"

"It's on this tape. I just know it."

"Maybe we should be like Dante and Virgil and get some sleep."

"You go ahead."

"Or maybe I should borrow your rosary and pray for Dorothy. You know, love thine enemies?"

"Not a bad idea. I'll stay here for a while."

Grace set the tape to repeat at normal speed. Her eyelids grew heavy, and her head sank to the kitchen table. She did not wake up till the eastern sky turned from black to blue.

Then, she woke up with a start. What time was it? Six in the morning? That meant three on the West Coast. There were no new voice messages but two emails from Father Flynn, saying that all other exorcism attempts had failed.

"Oh, damn, damn, damn!" Kathleen was sound asleep on the sofa. The children were still in their beds. Dante and Virgil were still.

Grace turned on the coffee maker and sat back down in front of her laptop. The tape kept repeating. She felt tears run down her face.

"How stupid I was not to consider this from the start. I should have realized that, for once, Larry was telling the truth. There was a demon. Not a natural cause but an actual demon that Larry let in. And not just into this house but into our whole world. And now we can't get rid of it. What more can we do? This thing has defeated us. Goddam you, Roach."

She looked at the screen again. In this part, you could see a line of contestants who had not yet sung. Dorothy was on the end. Grace enlarged Dorothy, who was speaking to the contestant next to her. Grace tried to lip-read.

"Dorothy? You feel all right?"

"I'm just a bit nervous. Excuse me. I'm going to the ladies' room."

"Sure. Let us know if you need anything."

Then Dorothy left the stage.

"Ooo-kay. Now let's say Dorothy is fully possessed by Roach. At that point. What could have taken place, which would upset a demon to the point of needing a bathroom break?"

Grace reversed the tape, then jumped from her chair and grabbed her cell.

"This is Father Flynn. I'm not in to take your call now, but if you will leave your name and number at the beep, I'll return your call as soon as possible."

"Father, this is Grace McGrath. There is a weak spot where we can hit Roach a lot harder. Now, I know it's a long shot. We have to try it! Please call me the instant you get this. Please!"

51

Three in the morning has been called the most unholy of hours. Scorch, flying high over the Hollywood Hills, set down on top of the second L in the Hollywood sign.

"Roach! How's it going?"

Roach, in Dorothy's form, did not look well. He seemed half-asleep, and drool was running out of Dorothy's mouth. A foul-smelling substance ran from beneath Roach down the stem of the Y. The naked Larry looked more dead than alive.

"Scorch?"

"It's me, bro. I got great news!"

"Whaaaat?"

"Satan accepted your terms! As soon as you get back to Hell with those two, he's going to turn time back. And get you Dante and Virgil. Oh, and you're getting your big parade. And the Distinguished Disservice medal! And remember when I messed up on the connector? Satan's taking that reprimand out of my personnel file."

"I keep thinking, who gave the exorcist my real name? It must have been Longianna Rae. I'm going to have to kill her."

"Yeah, right, later. What we have in our talons now is a bit more important."

"I don't feel too good," Roach moaned. "You see those three down there?"

"They're exorcists?" Scorch made an obscene gesture at them.

"Ye-es. The one in the middle has the big fat file. And they keep hitting me, Scorch! They have a tag team. And they keep hitting me, over and over again, and it hurts."

Scorch wanted to remind Roach that he should have known what would happen. And he would have known had he been paying attention during the antiexorcism classes. But he didn't. Scorch thought better of saying that. Not now.

"If we kill Larry and Dorothy right now, we're home free. What do you say? We can just let them drop."

"Scorch. Look down. There is a safety net. See?"

"Oh. Yeah. Why don't we reverse both of their heads and then drop them?"

"Because Larry and I are getting married tonight."

"Go on with you! You're not serious!"

"No. The wedding's tonight." Roach held up a floppy Larry Kavanaugh.

"Doesn't look like he'd be much fun in the sack, does he?"

"He'll perk up once I get him into Hell. They always do. I'll have him in chains and show him off to Dante and Virgil. They can write a few cantos about him. Hey, what are they going to throw at us now?"

Several more trucks approached the sealed-off site. They were from an upscale catering company in Beverly Hills. Workmen got out and began setting up a large tent.

"See, Scorch? We're winning. Must be that the tag team gave up on me. And now they're setting up for the wedding. Did you invite everyone?"

"Including Old Scratch himself? Yeah, sure."

"He can kiss my lovely bride."

"Looks like it will take a while to get this setup ready. Suppose those three start hitting on you again? Can you take any more?"

"They're giving up, see? And I can hold on a while longer. Look at them, Scorch. What are they compared to us? The Creator's biggest mistake! What do they accomplish? They get born, eat, excrete, make babies, die, and rot. Whereas, we! They are like dirt under our hooves. When you compare their frail, disordered lives to all that we are, you will see they are nothing! Go, Scorch, tell all of Hell the wedding is about to begin. And then back we go in time. All I have ever wanted is mine!"

52

By four in the morning, Roach was too weak to keep the rain falling. Not that it mattered. The tent was set up. Then more trucks arrived. Workmen unloaded chairs and placed them inside the tent.

By five, busses arrived full of people carrying cases. They vanished into the tent. They were followed by a black limo. Whoever or whatever was inside joined the crowd in the tent.

The eastern sky turned a trace of dark blue.

Lights went on inside the tent. Members of the Los Angeles Philharmonic unpacked their instruments and took their seats. The maestro stepped up to the podium.

The man coming out of the limo was the most obese that many had ever seen. The senior exorcist went up to him.

"Are you sure you can do this, Tony?"

"Father, I saw what was out there. It's horrible."

"Just close your eyes, Tony, and sing it for your mom."

"All right."

Roach started, when he heard the harpist render the first few notes. Then Tony took a deep breath and sang.

> *Ave Maria*
> *Gratia plena*
> *Maria, gratia plena*
> *Maria, gratia plena*

Roach threw back his head and screamed in agony.

> *Ave, ave dominus*
> *Dominus tecum*
> *Benedicta tu in mulieribus*
> *Et benedictus*
> *Et benedictus fructus ventris*
> *Ventris tuae, Jesus*
> *Ave Maria*

Two crashes followed. First Larry landed into the safety net, then Dorothy. The sun's corona rose over the Hollywood hills.

> *Ave Maria*
> *Mater Dei*
> *Ora pro nobis peccatoribus*
> *Ora pro nobis*
> *Ora, ora pro nobis peccatoribus*

Roach jumped to the top of the letter Y. "Turn back, my brothers! Turn back!" His scales melted and oozed down the Y. Then he took off into the rising sun.

> *Nunc et in hora mortis*
> *Et in hora mortis nostrae*
> *Et in hora mortis nostrae*
> *Et in hora mortis nostrae*
> *Ave Maria*

Larry, in a coma, was put into an ambulance and sent to Cedars-Sinai. The senior exorcist asked Dorothy her name.

"Dorothy Marie Walsh!" Then she too was on her way.

Thousands of miles distant, a cell phone in a kitchen table rang. "Grace? This is Cardinal Kelly. You were right. Your idea worked perfectly. Roach is gone."

"Roach? Gone?"

"Out of our world, directly to Hell, do not pass go."

The McGrath sisters fell onto the sofa, held on to each other, and shrieked.

"And you know what happens next?" Kathleen screamed at her sister.

"No! What?" Grace screamed back.

"Some man is going to take all the credit!"

53

"Keep moving, folks. There is nothing to see here."
That was the official advice of the city and county of Los Angeles. Quietly, the Hollywood sign was given a blessing. Not so quietly, it was power washed. Then all was as it had been before. Just keep going. Nothing happened here.

Sing! Sing! Sing! continued on schedule. Nothing was said about Dorothy. No more bets were placed. Everyone knew who was going to win.

Tony from Jersey City got the recording contract. He released a CD, which he titled *The Next Big Thing*. Tony went on to become one of the iconic recording artists of the twenty-first century.

Once back in Hell, Roach was placed in a solitary confinement cell. There was a bed, a sink, and a toilet, and a TV was mounted out of his reach. The same video played over and over again. Longianna Rae was speaking to the senior exorcist.

"'I am not Dorothy. The next person who calls me Dorothy dies! Don't you know that my name is Roach and I have long talons and strong fists?' That is what he said before he hit me."

The exorcist wrote it all down. "Roach? Are you sure that was what he said his name was?"

"No question. Roach is his name."

"I must say I have never heard of a demon by that name before."

"Neither have I," Longianna Rae admitted. "It's not like he was in *The Divine Comedy* or anything like that."

The video was set to replay for all eternity.

Larry and Dorothy would never be the same. Larry never really came out of his coma. Once back home, he was diagnosed as being in a chronic vegetative state. Cardinal Kelly had him placed in a nursing home run by the Divine Compassion nuns. He would live for twenty more years.

The sisters would remember that he had two of the most delightful children. They came to visit him twice each year, for Christmas and his birthday. Jeanine went to MIT. Bobby was in medical school at Georgetown. They told their father all their news, even though he never gave them any response.

What the nuns did not know was that this was the best relationship that Jeanine and Bobby ever had with their father.

On their final visit, Jeanine took her dad for a walk in the garden in his wheelchair. She stopped and exchanged greetings with a distinguished-looking older woman pushing a stroller. Inside the stroller, dressed in a white lace christening gown, was a plastic fetus.

"One of our more tragic cases," the mother superior told her. "She used to be a singer, and it's said she was once in Hollywood, on the verge of the big time. But since she has been here, she has not sung a note. She always joins the sisters for early-morning Mass. Then she tends to her baby."

"Has anyone told her that her baby is plastic?"

"We cannot. It would be cruel. Though there have been problems. Especially when she wanted to breastfeed her baby. But now she insists her baby has been weaned and is ready for solid food."

"Oh dear. What happens then?"

Mother Superior sighed. "All too often, we have Gerber's strained peas all over the place. When that occurs, we have to mop up the mess. Then she bathes her baby, puts a fresh diaper on it, and rocks it for a while. The poor soul has found a measure of peace. We can't complain."

Jeanine searched her memory. Wasn't there once someone on *Sing! Sing! Sing!* who had some history with her mother and Aunt Grace? It could well be, but that was so long ago. This was no megastar; this was only a shattered soul.

As the years passed, the entire incident got smaller in the rearview mirror. Nightmares grew rarer and ceased. Kathleen had always assumed that since she was the oldest, she would die first. It was a shock when Grace was the first of the McGrath sisters to go.

It was a hard loss. Kathleen had chosen not to remarry. "Enough of that!" she always said. But now her little Bobby was Robert J. Kavanaugh, MD. He was married and the father of three. Kathleen loved having his family so nearby. They moved into the new house at 7 Split Tree Circle.

Jeanine had the letters PhD after her name. The problem was she was so far away. At least there was a computer connection. Kathleen could place a terminal on the kitchen table, and it was like having her morning coffee with Jeanine. But not really the same.

That's why it was so hard not to have the real Jeanine around when her little sister made her transition. Jeanine could only virtually attend the funeral. Kathleen wanted to hold her and marvel at how much of Grace lived on in her.

But there was much to do to settle Grace's estate. Grace and Jeanine took the same size in clothing and shoes, so everything in Grace's closet was going to Jeanine. There were other things, too, that Grace treasured, including her rosary. Grace left a framed portrait of Dante and Virgil the cats as Dante and Virgil the poets.

There was also a handwritten note from the exorcist in Los Angeles. "I promise the McGrath sisters that I will not, as they say, hog all the credit. But I hope they will not mind my saying that it was beauty that killed the beast."

All these things Kathleen moved into a crate with the urn containing Grace's ashes and her marker. Grace would be buried so far away. This is what her little sister wanted.

"But, Mom!" the virtual Jeanine said. "Those shipping costs are an arm and a leg. I insist I'll help you pay."

Kathleen then addressed the crate to Jeanine, who had chosen to keep her old address. Actually, one could use any address one wanted at Jeanine's new home. So Kathleen printed out the shipping label.

Dr. Jeanine Kavanaugh
2 Split Tree Circle
Sally Ride Terran Colony
MARS

Bobby wheeled the crate to his pickup and drove Kathleen and his children to the UPS Spaceport.

His children were so eager to see a night launch. Kathleen was not so sure. She remembered the night launch that took Jeanine away. Jeanine still looked like a child, waving "Bye, Mom!" as if she were going to Alabama for space camp.

After paying the required arm and leg, Kathleen and her family went to the observation deck to see the crate loaded on a rocket. The rocket was due to leave after sunset. Kathleen decided to stay and watch. This would be a final farewell for Grace.

The countdown clock was a brilliant red in full darkness. Her grandchildren shouted out, "Five! Four! Three! Two! One! Liftoff! We have liftoff!"

Goodbye, my sister!

Again, the ground shook, and the scene lit up. As if at the beginning, when God said, "Let there be light."

And there was light. And it was good.

"Grandma? Why are you crying?"

"Pay me no mind. I'm just a silly old lady."

"Come on, Mom. Let's go home," Bobby offered. Kathleen needed to stay till the rocket became a small white dot and disappeared. Then she looked up at the night sky and heard Grace's voice one last time, reading her children a story.

Thence we came forth again, to see the stars.
… Inferno, Canto 34

ABOUT THE AUTHOR

Mary M. Schmidt was a student in Rome during the '60s, where she came to know of the feral cat colonies. She is an author of prose, poetry, and was a member of Poets Against the Iraq War. She currently lives outside of Annapolis with her cat, Graycie.